Abandoned

Books and Stories by Ron Mueller
The Taelo Series
Taelo: The Early Years
Taelo: The Golden Feather
Taelo: Journey of Discovery
Taelo: Dangerous Passage
Taelo: Condor Clan Slingers
Taelo: Circumvention
Taelo: The Journey of Sages
Taelo: Future Leaders Journey
Taelo: Collection

A Taelo Story
White Swan and Quiet Pheasant
The Child's Name
Floating Cloud
Quiet Rabbit
Busy Bee
Little Otter & Talking Wren
Broken Spear
Burley Bear & Meadow Flower

Science Fiction

The Savitar Series:
    Journey's End
    Savitar
    Confluence
    The Savitar Collection

Bram Nielson Series
    The Fold
    The Message
    Fold Wormhole
    Negative Fold
    Ripples in Time
    The Nielson Collection

Single Science Fiction Books
    Current Past and Future
    The Event
    The Door
    Viajante 7

Ron Mueller

<u>Fiction Series</u>
The Alex Evercrest Series
    The River Front
    The Girl on The Grill
    Missing
    Maggot
    Racist
    Votive Candles
    Windy City
    Country Road
    Pool of Blood
    Sins of the Daughter
    Body Parts
    The Skull Collector
    The Vanishing
    The Shadow Fighter
    Moonshine
    Grief's Trajectory
    The Magic Touch
    Nine Towers of Ku
    Abandoned
    Northern Lights
    Evercrest Collection One
    Evercrest Collection Two

A Brian Oneil Novel
    Hawaiian Phoenix
    Moon Curser
    Death Broker
    Brian Oneil Collection

The Problem Solver Series
    Solutions
    Drug Lords
    Border Crosser
    The Problem Solver Collection

Imagination by Courtney Huynh and Chloe Parker

Abandoned

Abandoned
By: *Ron Mueller*

Around the World Publishing LLC
4914 Cooper Road Suite 144
Cincinnati, Ohio 45242-9998

ISBN 13: 978-1-68223-958-2
ISBN 10: 1-68223-958-6

Distributed by Ingram
Model by: Pia @ShutterStock
Young Girl by: Phartisan@Dreamstime.com
Design by: Ron Mueller

Ron Mueller

Abandoned

<u>**Table of Content**</u>

Ron Mueller

Abandoned

Chapter 1: A Life Worth Escaping

Bento thought back over his life and realized that it had been one spent at the bottom of Brazilian society. His parents tried to give he and his eight brothers and sisters as good of a life as they could. Theirs was a hard life being servers of the wealthier. His mother was a maid to several families that were not necessarily rich, but they were well enough off to have a part time maid. His father was a laborer that was often unemployed and looked for day labor. They both worked hard to keep a roof over their head and keep everyone clothed and fed. They were firm but they never beat any of them.

He always figured their big mistake was having eight kids. He was the youngest. He got all the hand me downs in clothing. He was also often the one that got the least food when times were extra hard.

His tumbles with his brothers and sisters hardened him and he learned to get what he needed. He knew it had definitely shaped how he assessed those that he mixed with.

Ron Mueller

His schooling was spotty, but he did get through Ensino Médio, (secondary education). He was not a great student, and he did not like the school environment.

Then after getting out of school the reality of his situation hit him. No matter how hard he tried, he couldn't find a meaningful full-time job. To no avail he tried every means possible to land a job that paid well enough that he could move away from his parents and live on his own.

Then one of his school friends got him to become a "distributor" which was a fancy name for becoming a drug dealer. It turned out he was very good at being a distributor and was soon making enough money that he was able to enjoy some of the things in life that he had always seen others enjoying such as a day on the beach, eating at a restaurant, even dating. This made him become even better at distributing. He was soon rising in the ranks of the local drug ring. He was called in to meet with the two big bosses who congratulated him on his good sales and gave him a bigger territory to manage.

He was able to move into a much better neighborhood and into a decent apartment. Decent in that it was at least a step up from what he had been living in.

Not long after he met Janaina at a small local diner. He asked her out and soon they were dating on a regular basis. He was pleased that she was attracted to him. She had a knockout figure and her tanned white skin, black hair set her apart from other young women he had his eyes on.

Abandoned

It helped his ego that she said that he was the best-looking guy that she had ever thought of going out with. It was about a year later that he proposed.

His mother suggested he bring Janaina to dinner so that she and his dad could meet her.

That dinner turned out to be a catastrophe.

His mother was surprised and upset that Janaina was white. She let him know that she did not approve and didn't want mulatto or a pardos for a grandchild.

His father didn't say anything, but he did not come to his defense either.

It was clear that he was not going to get the approval of his parents, but he was not going to change his mind because they objected.

When he got married, his brothers and sisters attended his small wedding but neither of his parents showed up. Janaina had no relatives and there were only a few of her friends at the wedding. Almost all of the distributors that he managed were in attendance, which made him feel good since it showed him that he was doing a good job with them. He also realized that he truly was a drug dealer.

He was making enough that he could afford a small loft apartment, some new furniture and food was no longer an issue for him. It seemed that the two of them were headed into a good life.

Ron Mueller

Less than a year later, Janaina let him know that the was going to be a father.

This was good news, but it also bothered him.

Good news in that he wanted to be a father.

It bothered him that his child would someday find out that he was a drug dealer. He had become one of the top distributors and the big boss had put him in charge of several other distributors. His job was to make sure that those working for him gave him the right amount of money and that they kept only the cut they had agreed to. He was very good at making sure that those working for him were "honest."

Since all the sales money came to him and he took it into the office, he was often in possession of more money than most people made in a year.

The day came when he rushed Janaina to the hospital and waited outside of the delivery room. They had spent many hours looking at baby names and had selected one for a boy and one for a girl. It would either be Afonso if a boy or Aurea if a girl.

The nurse who came out let him know that he had a beautiful baby girl and that he could see her through the window in the nursery. He stood looking through the glass and what he though was the best-looking baby in the nursery.

He waited until she as carried out and followed the nurse to the room Janaina was in. He gave her a hug and then held Aurea for the first time. He though his heart was going to break because he was so happy.

Abandoned

A few days later, Aurea came home with Janaina. A home that now had a happy but worried father. He decided that he had to find a better life for his family than the one he had grown up in. He dutifully saved as much money as he could while he looked around for a way to escape his current role managing half a dozen distributors.

He was aware that he couldn't just tell his bosses that he was getting out of the distribution business. He was at a level where he had seen what happened to those that cheated or tried to move to another organization. Those people were somewhere pushing up grass and flowers. They could neither quit nor change allegiances. He did not see a way that he could possibly escape his current situation.

He was watching the news about a shooting in Cincinnati, Ohio and listened as a black female detective was being asked about the fact that she had solved a fifteen-year-old cold case and had saved the person who was now a young woman that had two children by her kidnapper. The story seemed to spark and light a fire within him. He had no idea where Cincinnati was located other than in the US, but he now had a goal. He would leave Brazil and go to Cincinnati. He would go where a black woman was seen as a heroine.

Ron Mueller

He found out where Cincinnati was located. He then found out how much it would cost to get there. His goal to save the astronomical amount and to get visas took him much longer than he anticipated. The time turned into years and his role in the drug distribution business continued to flourish.

Aurea's sixth birthday was the catalyst that finally and very loudly fired the starting gun. During the party she said that she wanted to be just like him.

"Just like him." "Just like him." "Just like him." Kept going through his mind. He didn't want any of his children to ever be just like him at least not the person that he currently had become.

He got the tourist visas for the US. He then skipped the payment on his apartment and arranged with Janaina to leave the country. He was short on the amount of money to pay for the airline tickets, but he had an upcoming money collection round that would give him what he needed and enough money to live for a few months in the US.

He figured that the amount of money did not matter. If he took it his fate would be the same no matter the amount. He made his collection rounds and headed straight to the airport where Janaina and Aurea were waiting for him.

He was constantly looking out for anyone that might be looking for him.

Abandoned

He was a wreck by the time that they got on the plane. He knew that he would be hunted but once on the plane he was able to relax and when the plane finally took off, he felt that he had made his escape. He doubted that anyone would learn where he had gone, and he was going far enough away that he figured no one would be sent after him.

The plane laned in Miami where they went through customs before going on to Cincinnati on a regional flight.

He was surprised that they landed in Kentucky at the Cincinnati International Airport. He got a ride to the hotel that he had rented that was on the western side of the city. He rented a room with two beds, for two weeks. On the same day as his arrival, he walked across to the other side of eighth street and got two jobs. One was as a short order cook and the other was managing the cash register at a gas station. He was surprised at how easy getting started was for him. He wondered about how long it would take to work his way up to some bigger, better paying jobs.

He asked Janaina to find as inexpensive an apartment to rent as possible and to get Aurea enrolled in school.

He was surprised at how quickly Janaina found a furnished two-bedroom apartment that was over a small restaurant in the downtown area. It was very basic and had mostly older furniture and appliances.

Ron Mueller

It was within walking distance to his two current jobs and the school where Aurea would go. This would allow him to continue working where he was until he could figure out how to get some better job or jobs.

He was impressed when Aurea took the school's entrance test and got placed one level above what he and Janaina expected. She had done so well that the principal commented that she was being placed one level above that was normal for her age, because her math and reading scores were so high that it was warranted. The principal also said that her verbal English skills were a little rough but good enough that she would have no problems.

Janaina was also very happy about everything. She had Aurea enrolled in school and she had talked herself into a part time job at the restaurant that was just below the apartment.

He was relieved that with their three incomes, they would be able to pay the rent, have enough money to buy food and be able to save for a rainy day. He figured that in a few months they would be in good financial shape.

The year flew by. There was little time for anything but work and more work. He made it a point that whenever he could the three of them did something together. They often went to the riverfront and enjoyed the free games that were available there and to have a picnic on the lawn.

Abandoned

On one occasion he splurged and rented a segway so that Aurea could experience riding it. They had a great time riding it together for a short time, but he was afraid that they might have a wreck.

During the summer they attended several free outdoor concerts where they sat on the hillside and enjoyed a picnic. Then during the winter, they made it to the ice-skating rink and all of them tried their luck on the ice.

Aurea was the one that seemed to be a natural. He and Janaina took off their skates and watched Aurea go around the rink. They held hands and smiled as they watched their beautiful daughter laughing and enjoying herself.

In the spring they walked across the Purple People's Bridge and when they got to the other side, he bought Aurea a bratwurst that they all ended up sharing.

He and Janaina agreed that their move to Cincinnati was the best decision they could have made.

Aurea spent almost all her extra hours at the main public library. Janaina had enrolled her in an after-school program that featured a variety of supervised activities. This allowed her to work at the restaurant while Aurea enjoyed herself in a safe environment.

It was a good year and it seemed that life for him and his family was on an upward path.

Ron Mueller

He was standing at the grill flipping a series of burgers when the cashier said that there was a rather tough looking dude at the counter asking to talk to him. He walked out and almost fainted when he saw Cristiano standing on the other side of the counter. He knew that Christiano was the mean partner of the drug distribution ring in Sao Paulo and if he was in Cincinnati, it meant trouble. He almost turned and ran but instead he faced Cristiano as if he had no fear when in fact, he was about to wet himself.

Cristiano spoke to him in Portuguese and asked him if he had the money that he had taken from his operation.

If the situation hadn't been so serious Bento would have laughed. He had spent the money and there was no money other than the little he and Janaina had been saving. That amount was a far cry from the money he had taken from the drug business. He knew if Christiano had personally made the trip he was there to make a point and to make an example of what happened when someone crossed the organization.

Christiano shook his head and smiled as he said that if he got his money back, he would only kill him but if that didn't happen, he would take some of that payment from Janaina before he killed her.

Abandoned

He figured that there was no money, so he said that he was also planning to cut out his tongue and cut off his ears, take them back to Sao Paulo and hang them behind the bar with a sign that declared that thieves were always caught and rewarded for their actions.

He asked what Bento had to say while he still had a tongue.

Bento stood silently as he thought about what he had to do.

Christiano nodded and said that he would be waiting out in the parking lot and that Bento should make it easy on himself. If he came out to the parking lot, he would kill him before cutting out his tongue.

Bento nodded and put up his hand and then turned and went back into the kitchen area. He did not stop at the grill but headed straight out the back door. He ran all the way back to the apartment.

Janaina had just returned from school with Aurea. She was surprised to see him and when she understood that they had been found she was as afraid as he was. She knew that they had to make a run for it, and she knew that they had to find a safe place to leave Aurea.

She said that they needed to get out of the apartment, and they needed to get Aurea to a safe place.

He convinced her that they would be safe until the next day.

Janaina said that she knew where they had to take Aurea and they had to do it very early the next morning.

Ron Mueller

A few hours before sunrise they all left the apartment with all the food they could carry and with Aurea's clothes, the few toys she had and a family picture of the three of them together in the park. It all fit in a large black plastic bag.

Aurea was confused about what was happening. She kept asking why they were walking across town in the dark.

Janaina led the way and crossed on the walking bridge that led to Mt. Adams. She was taking her to the only place she felt that Aurea would be safe. She did not know how she was going to be able to leave her there by herself, but she knew that she had to leave her and that she and Bento needed to try to make their escape afterwards.

She stood and looked up the three long series of steps that led to the house. She took Aurea up and had her sit on the porch swing with all her things. She then gave her a hug and let her know that she was loved but she had to stay here where she would be safe.

Bento knelt down and gave her a hug and repeated the fact that she was loved. He handed her a large envelope and said that she should give it to the lady that would come out on the porch later in the morning.

He looked at Janaina and said she should stay.

Abandoned

Janaina shook her head and said that Christiano had come for her as well. Back in Brazil he had often threatened to have her when she was through with her lover. He would just find her later, so she was going as well.

They both descended the steep steps and walked back to the downtown area.

They asked each other where they should go. They came to the realization that there was no place to run to.

They decided to have breakfast at the restaurant where Janaina worked and wait for the inevitable.

They had just finished their breakfast when Christiano walked in. He looked around and asked if he could join them at their table. He smiled and asked if they were ready for a ride out to the countryside. He then asked where their lovely daughter was and when he got no answer he simply said "good" I have no interest in her.

He stood up and said they should follow him.

The owner came out and asked if everything was OK.

Janaina smiled, said that she appreciated his concern, but everything was fine as she gave him a hug and then followed Christiano out to the car.

The owner followed but stayed in the doorway. He took a picture of the license plate and stepped back inside. He figured he had enough of his own problems and didn't need to get involved in his employee's problems. He suspected that they were in the country illegally.

Christiano instructed her to sit in the back and let her know that he had a gun that would be aiming at Bento if she tried anything.

He then got on seventy-one, drove several exits past King's Island before exiting and driving through the farm country. Then at a sign that declared that the road was to be used by only authorized personnel, he turned and went into the forest. He hoped that it would not be used while he was having the graves dug and he was covering them up.

He stopped the car and instructed the two of them to get out and walk around to the front of the car. He screwed on a silencer as he walked around to meet them.

Janaina saw what he was doing and as fast as she could she ran towards him. She hoped to knock him down so that Bento could kill him.

Bento realized what she was doing and rushed after her.

Christiano barely had time to finish putting on the silencer before he was hit and knocked back a step by Janaina. He shook his head and said "muito ruim para você" and shot her between the eyes.

Bento thought he was going to get a chance at taking Christiano down when he felt the bullets hit him in the chest. He gave Christiano a finger and then the world went black.

Christiano shook his head when realized that he would need to dig the graves to bury the two. He had planned to have the two dig their own graves.

Abandoned

He put on his rubber gloves, cut off Bento's ears, his tongue and put them into a plastic bag between aluminum foil and sealed it. He dropped the bag into a US priority mail envelope that he would mail when he got to the airport.

He found a place where a natural dip in the land provided some initial depth and then he went to work. He decided that one grave would be sufficient. He put them both in, covered the grave, made sure there was a rock layer across the top and then put old leaves and some tree branches over all of it. He stepped back and decided that it would never be found.

Not far from the grave he found a large flat rock and put the gun under it. It was a gun that he had paid for in cash on the street and would never be traced to him even if it was found.

He then left but before reaching the highway, he threw the shovel into the ditch.

He felt justified and successful as he drove back to the airport.

A short time later, he drove into the car rental and a few moments after that he rode the shuttle back to the terminal. Once inside he dropped his envelope into the mailbox then walked up to the check-in counter. He was not flying directly back to Brazil but was flying west to visit the Grand Canyon and then walk out on the see through walkway that would give him a look down into the canyon. He also planned to visit Bryce canyon and enjoy a hike before flying to Mexico City where he would spend several days and then fly back to Sao Paulo.

He figured that he might as well mix some pleasure with business. The business had been quickly done and the pleasure, though brief was what he was on his way to do.

He looked forward to getting back to Sao Paulo and a relaxing time there. He hoped that the mail would get there before him.

Abandoned

<u>Chapter 2: The Package on the Porch</u>

Matt was still out with the EMT team, but Alex figured he would be arriving shortly. She was ready to prepare breakfast and was waiting until he arrived. She had invited Johnnie to join them and afterwards they would take their normal ride into work.

She hoped that Matt had an easy night, but she knew that was seldom the case. He told her the time right after the closing of the bars usually was peak time for his team to make several runs from some accident to the nearest hospital.

The doorbell rang and she figured that Johnnie had arrived. She went to the door and opened it.

She was not surprised to see Johnnie, but he was holding a bulging black bag in one hand and had his other hand on the shoulder of a beautiful, auburn-haired young girl who looked to be frightened.

He commented that she had been sitting on the porch swing and said that her mother and father had dropped her off where she would be safe.

Alex knelt down and asked the young girl her name and learned that it was Aurea. She then asked Aurea why her parents had left her on the porch.

"Because they wanted me kept safe and you are the only one, they trusted to keep me safe," Aurea quietly replied. She gave the envelope she had in her hand to Alex and said that her mother said that it was for her.

Alex accepted the envelope looked in it expecting to find a note and was surprised that it did have a note, but it was also filled with one-hundred-dollar bills. She looked up at Johnnie and asked what was in the black bag.

He put it down, looked into it and replied that it looked like clothes and a few other odd and ends.

Alex asked Aurea to follow her and as she led the way to the kitchen she asked if Aurea would like to have some breakfast.

She had Johnnie put the bag down just outside of the kitchen door.

She handed the envelope to Johnnie and asked him to count the amount of money in it.

She offered Aurea some eggs, pancakes, and a lot of syrup.

That got a smile from Aurea.

Alex asked when her parents would be back to pick her up.

Johnnie chuckled and said that given what was in the bag and the money in the envelope he figured it might be a long time.

Alex was trying to figure out what to do when Matt walked in from the backyard.

Abandoned

He smiled and said that he wasn't expecting company for breakfast.

Alex gave him a hug and introduced Aurea who had been dropped off on their front porch for safe keeping.

Alex asked him to sit down, and she would get him his breakfast.

Matt sat down and started a conversation with Aurea.

Alex knew from past experience that kids normally liked Matt and Matt had a natural way of talking to them.

He first asked her for her mother's and father's name. He asked where she was from and learned that they had come from Sao Paulo. He learned that they had been in Cincinnati almost a year.

He soon knew what school she was attending and the names of her teachers. He learned that her favorite place was the library where she normally spent her after school time. She liked the River Front Park because there were free games. He found out the address where she and her parents lived.

Alex kept quiet as she wrote down what she was hearing.

Johnnie joined her and asked what she was planning to do about the situation.

She replied that she was going to take the day off to find out what was going on.

Johnnie offered to help and suggested that he call Mary and ask her to come over to watch Aurea while the two of them investigated the situation. He added that Matt needed to get to bed and get some rest since he had been out the entire night.

Alex thought for a minute and then said that if Mary didn't mind her help would be greatly appreciated.

Johnnie gave a little laugh and commented that Mary would most likely love to do it. He walked out into the backyard and made a call. A short time later he walked back in with Mary.

Matt finished his breakfast and thanked Aurea for sharing her time with him. He looked at Alex and asked if she had the situation covered and smiled when he saw her mouth a thank you to him. He nodded and said he was going to take a shower and then get a good night's sleep.

Aurea asked who was going to take her to school.

This was something that Alex had not thought about.

Mary sat down at the table and asked where she went to school. She said that she would take her and asked when she had to be there.

Mary looked at Alex and asked if she had the right idea of why she had been called.

Alex nodded and said that if Mary could accompany Aurea and find out her routine it would be a great help. She added that all expenses would be paid. She also asked if she could get one of the guest bedrooms ready for Aurea.

Abandoned

Johnnie pointed to the black bag and said that he figured everything that she had was in the bag.

Mary opened the black bag, looked into it, and let out a whistle. She reached in and took out a framed picture of Aurea and her parents. She handed it to Johnnie and said the picture might come in handy.

Alex walked out of the kitchen to the back porch and called the Chief. She informed him of the situation and let him know that she was going to treat the situation like a case, but she was going to take the day off to do so.

He said that she did not need to use her vacation and that he wanted her to come in and that he wanted Trey to join her in her investigation. He made the point that parents dropping off their child on a strangers porch was very unusual and he figured the situation merited handling it like an actual case that needed to be investigated.

She agreed to come into the office with Johnnie and to get things organized.

When she went back into the kitchen, Johnnie asked her if she planned to eat breakfast.

She shook her head and said that the two of them should plan to ride to work and figure out what the next step would be.

She went to the drawer in the kitchen and took out several hundred dollars and gave it to Mary and told her to use a taxi and spend whatever she needed but to get receipts because the situation might turn into an actual case.

Ron Mueller

Mary looked at the amount of money and shook her head and asked what she thought a taxi was going to cost.

Aurea asked if Alex was going to find her parents.

Alex sat down at the table and put her hands on Aurea's hands and said that she was going to do everything possible to find them but while she was looking Aurea would be staying in a room in the house and would be kept safe. She should plan on going to school, then to the library afterwards and that later they would all have dinner either at the house or at a restaurant.

She then said that she and Johnnie were leaving, and that Mary was going to make sure she got to school and afterwards to the library.

She looked at Mary and asked her to find out what she could from the teachers and the librarians.

She followed Johnnie down the front steps to where they had their bikes chained.

The two talked back and forth via their headsets on their ride down the hill to the police station.

Once there, Alex stopped to get her cup of coffee before heading over to her desk.

She knew she was in for a quiz when Trevor smiled and asked why she was late for work.

Trey handed her half of a bear claw, and she slowly took a bite before replying to Trevor.

Johnnie walked in with his coffee, looked into the donut box, and picked out a glazed cake donut.

Abandoned

She smiled and replied to Trevor's question that she had been looking for a suitable case that they could work on, and she was going to make sure he got the exciting end.

Trevor laughed and said that he had never figured out what end the dull part of any of her cases happened to be.

The Chief came over and suggested that she, Johnnie, and Trey accompany him into his office.

Bill laughed and said that it seemed that they were going to be left out.

The Chief looked over to him and said that he should be glad to be able to relax while he ate his donut and had his coffee.

Once in the office, the Chief asked Alex to explain the situation. He made the point that parents dropping kids off to a stranger for safe keeping was very unusual. He stated that he was going to treat it as a formal case that involved potential danger. He said that he had already informed his bosses and they all agreed that given the history of your cases it was warranted.

Alex shook her head and asked what they meant by the history of her cases.

He asked her how many times she had been shot and ended up in the hospital.

She nodded and said that it was more times than she cared to think about.

He handed her the folder that was labeled, "The package on the front porch case."

She read the label and laughed. She said that it was the most beautiful package that she had recently seen. It had dark brown eyes, auburn hair, and a honey-colored skin and it was well composed and polite. She knew she was from Brazil but had yet to follow up on that.

The Chief smiled and said that she should make sure that she did not get too attached to that beautiful package.

He asked her how she planned to proceed.

She said that the place she was going to start was the hole in the wall diner just a few blocks away. Then she was going to the Cincinnati Library and talk to some librarians and finally she was going to walk to where Aurea went to school and see if she could talk with Aurea's teachers. She said that by the late afternoon she hoped to figure out how she would proceed.

She added that she had Mary was looking after Aurea and probably talking to some of the same people.

The Chief then asked if she planned to leverage the rest of the team.

Alex smiled and said that she would love to as soon as she had something for them to do but at the moment, she was not sure what that might be.

He nodded and looked at Trey and simply said, "have her back."

Trey smiled and asked if he meant "hold her back."

The Chief laughed and said for him to do both.

Abandoned

Alex smiled, waved her case folder, and walked out of the office.

She walked over to where Bill and Trevor were sitting having their morning coffee and asked them if they wanted to come along and enjoy brunch at a small local restaurant.

Trevor nodded and said that he would love to but that she had to lead the way into the restaurant because he did not want to be asked along just to serve as a shield.

Bill gave Trevor a shove and said that the next time bullets flew he was going to stand behind him.

Alex led the team to the small restaurant. She and Johnnie had made it a point to try breakfast and lunch at almost all the downtown establishments. This particular one had been visited once but had never made it to their favorite list.

She walked in and was greeted by the same person who had served her before. She asked for a table for five.

He smiled and said that he was pleased that she had decided to come back. He asked her to be patient because his normal waitress was absent.

Alex put in her order for tea and a scone and once the orders were in, she asked where the waitress that was absent had gone.

The owner said that she and her husband had an early morning breakfast and as they were finishing a large rather rude man came in and spoke to them in a foreign language. Then the waitress got up gave him a hug and followed the man out to his car.

He said that he followed them out to door, and that he got a picture of the license plate. He pulled out his phone and pulled up the picture.

Johnnie took the phone and sent the picture to all of them. He looked over at Trevor and asked him to follow up on it.

Alex asked the proprietor what language the rude person had used.

He shook his head and said that it was not Spanish but seemed similar.

A few moments later, Trevor's phone buzzed. He kept saying, "yes, yes, OK," and then hung up.

He looked around and said that the car was a rental that had been rented at the airport.

Alex asked that he and Bill follow up and see if it was still out and if not see if they could find out to what airline the renter had gone to. She added that the car should be impounded so that forensics could go over it in detail and get fingerprints and DNA.

Trevor nodded and said that he was glad that so far, he and Bill got the easy end of the case.

Alex smiled and said that they should get going while the trail was hot and to make sure neither of them got shot.

Once they had left, she looked at Trey and Johnnie and said that she was beginning to think that they would not find Aurea's parents alive. She hoped that she was wrong but to have someone come to Cincinnati from Brazil to meet with them felt ominous to her.

Abandoned

She wondered what the two had been running from. She looked at Johnnie and asked if he could look them up on some database that would have their visa information. And if he could follow their names to wherever it might lead.

She was quiet for a moment then asked Trey whether she could bring Aurea to his grill out on Sunday.

Trey nodded and said that he had just gone through all the toys that Nolan had outgrown. He was planning to pass them on to friends or give away. He figured he had plenty that might interest Aurea but there would be no kids her age to play with at the grill out.

Alex smiled and said that Matt was coming along and would fill in.

She then suggested they go to the library and see what they could learn there.

Johnnie nodded, said that he still had many librarian friends that he was sure would have noticed Aurea and might have some information that might prove useful.

Several librarians knew Aurea and commented that she was a bright young girl that must have been related to Johnnie because she always made sure to attend the lectures that had refreshments provided.

That gave Johnnie a laugh. He added that no one as pretty as Aurea would be a relative of his.

He asked what other things that Aurea was into and learned that Aurea loved to do research on the internet and by research she was into researching famous individuals and the histories of various countries.

Trey asked if that was common for someone so young and learned that it was not and that was why it was being mentioned.

Alex asked about Aurea's parents and learned that Aurea's mother would sign her in and then leave for work. She would return on time to sign Aurea out and take her home. It was clear that the mother took very good care of her daughter and the two of them were close.

Alex thanked each of the librarians and then took a moment to summarize that they had learned that Aurea loved the treats she could get at the library, and she was into learning about the history of the world around her. She added that the treats would be attractive to any kid but Aurea arranged her time so she could enjoy one each day. She was also a serious young lady in that she was into studying history and famous people.

Back in the office, Johnnie focused on getting into the database that would have the visa information for Aurea's parents. He also ran the face recognition program against the news databases in Sao Paulo. It did not take long for him to find a couple of articles that had Bento's picture. Several times he was standing behind the ring leaders of a drug distribution ring that controlled most of Sao Paulo.

Abandoned

Once again Alex commented that she was feeling more and more like they would not find either Janaina or Bento alive. She wondered if either of the two ring leaders might be the one that had left the diner with the two.

She asked Johnnie to go back with a picture of the two and see if the diner's proprietor recognized either of them. She also asked him to send the pictures out to Bill and Trevor to see if any of the ticket agents recognized either of the two.

She led the way to the school that Aurea attended and once there she introduced herself and the fact that she was trying to find out what she could about Aurea's mother and father. She did not learn much but was asked to clarify the fact that Aurea was accompanied to school by a Mary Higgins, and she wanted confirmation that everything was legal and appropriate.

Alex assured her that Aurea was being looked after while she tried to locate her mother and father.

She was then able to talk to several of the teachers that had nothing but praise for Aurea, her behavior, and her high standing in all of her classes.

She unexpectedly felt sense of pride in the positive information she was learning about Aurea.

After returning to the office, she was sitting at her desk when Bill and Travis returned from the airport and said that they had struck pay dirt in that one of the ticket agents recalled one of the men in the pictures and called him a rude dude because he was upset that he couldn't get a first-class seat.

He was headed for the Grand Canyon and was traveling on a one-way ticket. The agent conjectured that he must be leaving from that airport on a ticket of some other airline but when he had asked about helping to make a good connection, he had been told to mind his own business.

Alex asked Trevor and Bill if they wanted to join in on an evening dinner at a restaurant of Johnnie's choice.

Both of them said that they had other plans for the evening.

Trey spoke up and said that he preferred to go home to dinner.

Matt was still out with his EMT team at dinner time, so Alex, Johnnie, Mary, and Aurea went to dinner at a restaurant that had a great view of the River Front Park's play area and the John A. Roebling Suspension Bridge that crossed the river to Covington.

Aurea was immediately drawn to the window and said that she saw a couple of places where she had played. She turned away from the window and then asked whether Alex had found her mother.

Alex said that she had not.

After ordering dinner, Alex shared the fact that everyone that she had talked to had said nice things about Aurea. She asked Aurea if she would like to go with her and Matt to a grill out at Trey's house.

Aurea asked if there would be any other kids there.

Abandoned

Alex shook her head and said that there would be no kids but plenty of toys, an outdoor swing set and plenty of great food.

Aurea nodded and said, "OK."

Ron Mueller

Abandoned

<u>Chapter 3: A Call of the Heart</u>

Johnnie continued tracking Christiano's travel but the trail was cold. Christiano left the country for Mexico City just ahead of when Johnnie found out where he was. Once out of the country, Johnnie knew that the final destination would be Sao Paulo. He let Alex know and then began to see how he could find a computer trail to him. Alex let everyone know that for the moment Christiano had successfully made his escape. She contacted her friend the "Angel on the Hill" and asked if any of the cartels were supplying drugs to Christiano and the distribution ring that he operated in Sao Paulo. It was not long before she learned that indeed a large amount of drugs went that way. She was not sure what she would do with that information, but it confirmed the drug connection. She would keep that in mind as she thought about how to get to him.

She asked Bill to get the mileage that the rental car was used after Christiano rented it. She discussed this with Trey and Johnnie and after deducting the mileage to and from downtown Cincinnati from the Airport there were about seventy to seventy-five unaccounted miles. She went forty miles up both interstate seventy-five and seventy-four and looked where she ended up. She tapped on the screen in the area where that mileage ended and said that she thought they would find the bodies somewhere off of highway seventy-four because it had the most forested area.

The problem as she saw it was that they would be hunting blind over a very large, wooded area. She asked if anyone had any ideas.

Johnnie raised his hand and said, "Vultures."

Trevor laughed and asked if he expected the bodies to be laying out in some field where the vultures would see them.

Johnnie shook his head and said that vultures had an acute sense of smell and would probably be able to get the scent even from a buried body. He added that they should pay attention to the vultures circling over the established cemeteries.

He suggested that they contact the forest service and see if they would check out specific areas below any circling vultures in the area that they suspected the bodies might be.

Abandoned

Alex laughed, said that it was a great idea and that she hoped that the forest service would think so as well since she would be asking them to look skyward to find circling vultures. She made several calls and got in touch with the service. She shared the case she was on and that a drug enforcer might have killed two individuals and buried them somewhere in a fairly large area and she had no other idea than to see if the vultures might be sensitive enough to smell the bodies that would be buried somewhere in the woods.

She agreed with the ranger that it was a long shot but did get his agreement to have his personnel keep an eye on the vultures and explore the ground beneath where they were circling.

He said he was only doing it because he had followed a couple of her cases and knew that she had solved some very weird ones. He said that if his folks found anything he would contact her, but she had to promise to highlight his organization for the help they might provide.

Alex laughed and said that she would be glad to give all the recognition to him and his organization. She added that she didn't need her department tagged with using vultures to solve their cases.

Trevor laughed and said that the team had use just about every other means to solve their cases and many of those other means had come about because of Johnnie. He pointed over to him and said the if vultures worked, he would personally buy him a lunch at any restaurant in town.

Alex went into the weekend having done all she could do. She didn't have much to show for her efforts but didn't know what else to do. This frustrated her and she planned to spend extra time on the treadmill.

She decided to focus her efforts on Aurea. That afternoon after school she asked Auria if she liked to bike ride.

Aurea said that she did but that she hadn't had a bike to ride since they had come to Cincinnati.

Alex said they should go to a bike shop and see if they had any bikes that would be Aurea's size.

During the short ride to the bike shop Alex asked Aurea to share some of her memories from Brazil.

Aurea said that she knew that she and her parents lived in Capão Redondo which she knew was a poor section of Sao Paulo. She added that though they were poor she got to attend school and they often went to the beach in Santos. Her father had said that soon they would be moving to a better neighborhood but before that happened, he said they were instead coming to the US.

Since Alex knew that Bento had been part of a drug distribution gang, she figured that he had arranged his departure using the money that passed through his hands. Getting the money back or just getting rid of the person who took it was probably why Cristiano had come to Cincinnati.

Abandoned

She thought of the vultures and wondered how long a body had to decompose before the vultures would be able to get the scent.

They arrived at the bicycle shop and her favorite bike mechanic, Sam, greeted her. He asked if she had brought one of her bikes in and learned that she wanted to buy a bike.

He commented that she had three of his best bikes and wondered what she would do with a fourth.

Alex held Aurea in front of her and said that it was for her.

He nodded and said that he had several that would be just right for her and led them to the four bikes he had in mind.

Alex looked them over and said that the two that had multiple gears would most likely be the ones that would allow Aurea to keep up with her and Matt.

She asked Aurea which of the two bikes she liked best.

Aurea asked if she could really have one of them. She looked over one that was a vibrant pink and shook her head and said that it was too girlish. She asked if she could try out the black one.

Sam pushed the bike out the front door to the large parking lot in front of the store. He had Aurea straddle the bike and adjusted the seat to Aurea's height and leg length.

Aurea pushed off and expertly got on. She struggled with changing gears but soon got the hang of that. She rode around the lot several times.

Her laughter and bright smile was all that Alex needed. She let Sam know that he had made a sale.

Sam commented that Aurea seemed to be a natural. He put the bike on the rack on Alex's car and then led the way back into the store. He asked who Aurea was and why she was buying a bike for her.

Alex said that it was a complicated story but she was currently charged with taking care of Aurea and she wanted her to participate with her and Matt and some of the things she enjoyed so she was buying her a bike so she could do so.

Sam nodded and said that for that brief explanation he was giving her a ten percent discount.

Alex thanked him and said that it was almost time to bring her three bikes in for their annual tune up and parts replacement. She went ahead and scheduled that and then led the way out of the store.

Aurea walked to the back of the car and ran her hands along bike's fenders and asked if the bike was really to be her own.

Alex laughed and said that it was too small for her so, yes it was hers.

Alex asked if Aurea had any other outfits to go out riding.

Aurea said that she only had one set of pants to wear.

Alex said that she was going to take her shopping in a special place. She then drove to the Goodwill Store where she always went when she needed a new outfit. She always bought her work outfits there because of the very reasonable price that she normally was able to find.

Abandoned

Once they were inside and looking for some jeans and other suitable riding pants, Aurea commented that her mother had taken her to a store that was much smaller but that was very similar that had good prices on all the things in the store. She asked if this was the same kind of store.

Alex said that it was and that she came shopping whenever she needed a new outfit to wear to work.

Aurea said that she thought Alex was rich and wondered why she would shop at a store for poor people.

Alex replied that she was not rich, and the store was not just for poor people. She had a good job that she liked, and she had a nice home, but she felt like she was a person that managed her money so that she could also help others.

They left the store with several outfits for Aurea that made sure she would have enough play and school clothes.

Alex said that there was one more special place they needed to stop before they went back home.

She pulled into her favorite ice cream shop and led the way in.

She pointed to the board and said that every choice was a good choice and Aurea should choose the flavors and suggested get only two scoops because the scoops were large.

Aurea looked at the board for a long time and said that there were too many choices.

Alex laughed and said that she agreed and that they would have to come back many times until they had tried them all.

Once they had their ice cream she led the way to a table in the corner.

She asked what else Aurea remembered about Brazil.

Aurea said that she remembered her grandmother who she knew was mad at her father because he had chosen to marry her mom. She had been kind the few times they had met but it was always for a short time. She also knew that her dad's last job paid more but it was not a nice job because she heard her grandmother arguing with him about it. After that she never saw her grandmother again.

Alex could image the grandmother realizing that her son was a drug dealer and getting mad about it. She wondered how that mother would feel when she learned that her son had been killed by the people that he had worked for when he had tried to escape that life.

Alex shook her head and told herself to stop jumping ahead of what she knew for sure. She had no bodies, so she had nothing but conjecture in her hands. She watched Aurea enjoying her ice cream. It had only been a couple of days, but she knew that she was already getting too close. It was not going to be easy to step back from what she was feeling if her mother and father were found alive.

She shook her head as the thought about relying on vultures to find Aurea's parents.

Abandoned

She and Aurea got back to the house a short time before Matt was to get home. The plan was to go for a bike ride before going out to dinner.

She would make sure that she adjusted her dinner reservations at the Riverside Inn to include Aurea. She was sure that the view and barbeque would be something that Aurea would enjoy.

Matt arrived home right on time and said that he had a bike ride's worth of energy left but that going to dinner would need to be via taxi.

He asked if Aurea fit on any of their bikes and smiled when Aurea said that she had a new one of her own.

He looked at Alex and asked if she had been to the bike shop and how many extra hours was, she going to make him work for that visit.

Aurea took his hand and asked if he was the one that had to pay and that she hoped that he did not have to work too long.

Matt knelt down, gave her a hug, said that he was just joking and that they should all get ready for a nice ride. Then later they would enjoy a nice dinner together.

Alex coached Aurea on the ride down the steep streets and said that going down was difficult because they had to use the brakes but coming back from the ride would be harder because they would all end up pushing their bikes back to the house.

The ride on the bike trail allowed Alex to talk to Matt. She asked him what he thought about having a daughter like Aurea.

Matt looked at her and asked if she was seriously contemplating taking Aurea in.

Alex nodded and said that there was something about the situation that seemed to be calling to her. She asked him again about Aurea.

Matt smiled and said that he liked her as well but that he was going to wait until the case was closed before giving his answer to the question. He did not want his heart in one place if Aurea's mother was found alive and things had to change.

Alex said that was fair because she had the same reservations.

She reminded him that in two weeks they would be going up to see her parents and that by that time he might have to give her an answer.

Matt laughed and said that he knew she always solved her cases in lightening fashion and that he would get himself ready for such an event. He smiled and said that it would be an easy decision.

The ride as always seemed to relax Alex and when they returned the way back up the hill was not as hard as she had made out and Aurea was able to pedal up much of the way.

Matt said that he was game to walk down to the restaurant, but he was sure that he did not want to walk back up to the house.

They all went to get a quick shower. Aurea commented that she knew she was living in rich person's home because she had her own shower.

Abandoned

Alex smiled and said that she had to share hers with Matt and he was really a big guy.

Matt laughed and said that he would make room in the shower any time she wanted to join him.

They left and walked down the hill with Aurea holding both of their hands as they walked along. She chattered all the way to the restaurant about how much fun the ride had been. Alex looked up at Matt who just smiled and shook his head.

They were seated with a great view of the river. Alex suggested sharing a slab of ribs but each of them should have their own baked potato with all the trimmings.

Aurea looked at both of them and said that she was beginning to think that they were really rich people who didn't know they were rich.

Alex nodded and answered that maybe she and Matt would need to rethink their status.

On the ride back from the restaurant Aurea fell asleep sitting between the two of them.

Alex instructed the taxi driver to drop them off on the street above the address she had given her. This allowed them to carry Aurea in via the back yard that was at that level.

They carried her to her bedroom that Mary had arranged. It seemed that Aurea had been using it for some time even though it had only been a few days.

After getting her into her bed, Alex led the way to their bedroom and said that she was going to get ready for bed and that she planned to sleep in late.

Matt gave a little laugh and asked if that meant getting up by seven in the morning.

When she awoke, Alex looked at the clock and saw that Matt had been right. It was only seven in the morning, and she was ready to get up.

She was in the kitchen getting things ready for breakfast when Aurea walked in and asked if there was something to eat.

Alex gave her a hug and said that after watching her eat the night before she didn't think she would need to eat for another week.

Aurea sat down at the table and put her head down on her arm and said that she could wait until later.

Alex asked if some warm oatmeal with golden raisins and honey drizzled on top and a cup of warm milk sounded like something she might want.

Aurea nodded her head.

Alex got her the oatmeal and microwaved a cup of milk to warm it up. She then sat down with her cup of coffee and a bowl of oatmeal. She peeled an orange and put the sections on a small plate at the center of the table.

Aurea was almost done eating when Matt walked in and said that he hoped that the two of them had left him a little bit for him to eat.

Abandoned

There was a knock on the back door.

Alex let Mary and Johnnie in.

Mary put a plate with a loaf of banana bread that she had already sliced in the middle of the table.

Alex thanked her as she got up and got the butter out. She buttered a slice and put it on a plate for Aurea.

She then did the same for herself. A warm wave of pleasure seemed to flow through her as she realized that she was totally into having Aurea at her table.

Later that evening, she, Matt, and Aurea sat in the family room reading. Aurea had brought home several books from the library. She was starting to read <u>The Adventures of Huckleberry Finn</u> by Mark Twain.

Alex poked Matt and pointed to the book Aurea had in her hands.

Matt only smiled, nodded, and quietly said that she was definitely reading above age level.

Aurea looked up at them and said that she was just an old person in disguise and flipped to the next page.

That got a chuckle from both of them.

It was only a few hours later when they arrived at Trey's house for the barbeque. Lesley gave Aurea a hug and said that she had invited a neighbor and his family to the barbeque, because they had a daughter the same age and the two of them could have the run of the back yard and tackle any of the games available in the basement.

She took Aurea by the hand and walked with her to the backyard where she introduced her to Pattie and suggested they use the swing set, or they could get whatever they wanted to eat or go to the basement and play any games they wanted to play.

Lesley came back onto the porch where Alex was sitting and commented that Aurea was the beauty that Trey had described.

Alex shared what Aurea was reading.

Lesley laughed and said that Alex was acting like a proud mother boasting about how smart her daughter happened to be. She asked whether Alex was getting prematurely serious about the situation.

Alex nodded and said that she probably was. She and Matt had talked about having kids, but she had been afraid of getting pregnant because of the number of times she had been shot. It had made her hesitate about having kids.

She added that she was sure that Aurea would need a home. There was no way that she would let her be placed in the foster care service and she had learned that though there was a grandmother in Brazil there had been little connection between her and Aurea. If it came to it she would figure out what it would take to get the grandmother to relinquish any claim to Aurea.

She said that as soon as she was sure that Aurea was an orphan she would put in the paperwork to be her legal guardian until she could work through the adoption process.

Abandoned

Lesley took hold of Alex's hands and said that she hoped that everything would work out as Alex was anticipating and added that she and Trey would be on hand to help.

Alex thanked her and said that she did not want to find out that Aurea's parents had been killed but things were looking that way.

Ron Mueller

Abandoned

<u>Chapter 4: Trip Home</u>

Alex called home and let her mother know that on her and Matts visit they would have a surprise for her and that she would never be able to guess what the surprise might be.

Rose-Anne knew that her daughter was always into something and that she most often had no way to guess what that might be. She responded that as long as it did not involve thugs trying to shoot their way into the house as they had done on a previous visit, she was looking forward to any surprise that Alex might have. She asked how many other people would be coming with her because she had also been surprised when it seemed that she had invited everyone she knew to come over to the house for dinner.

Alex said that only one other person other than Matt would be coming. She added that going out fishing would be one of the activities that she wanted to do but otherwise sitting around the pool was as exciting as she wanted the visit to be. She asked if coming in the middle of the week would work. She was happy to get an OK.

Rose-Anne said that she was working from home and that any day during the week would work. She asked whether she should plan for a formal dinner or if anything that she had ready to eat would work.

Alex said that she should not cook a formal dinner and that anything for lunches and dinners would work. She wanted to take it easy and wanted to go out fishing at her favorite spot on the lake.

Visiting her mother a few days early allowed her to get out of the office before she went crazy. The case seemed not to be making any progress and that was really bothering her..

Matt had let her know that he would be off Wednesday and Thursday and that going to Evanston would work as long as he was back by late afternoon on Friday.

That fit exactly what Alex wanted. She figured that she would get Aurea out of school and the three of them could fly out early on Wednesday.

At work she was frustrated by the lack of progress, and she knew that she was driving everyone crazy trying to figure out what they could do next.

The rental car was in the impound lot where Bill and Travis had followed the thorough examination that had been done. They got fingerprints that matched both Janaina and Bento and a third set of prints that Johnnie was trying to track down on the Brazilian data base but figured it would match that of Cristiano.

Abandoned

Johnnie said that breaking into the Sao Paulo police data base had been easier than he had anticipated and that he would soon have Cristiano's prints verified. He said that he would see what else he could dig up on he had his partner.

Trevor had chosen to tone down his teasing because he sensed that this case had become very personal to Alex. He and the team had talked, and they all realized that Alex had gone way past the line of not getting personally involved. They all agreed that having Aurea live in her house was like baiting a mouse with cheese or anyone of them with a free ticket to a ballgame. They were all in agreement that when they found Aurea's parents, they would not be alive but so far, they had no break in the case.

The Chief noted Alex's tense behavior. He noticed that the normal back and forth among the team was also absent. At home he talked to Mary-Anne about the situation and followed her advice to say nothing at work unless Alex broke out of her normal control mode. She said that saying nothing was probably the best he could do.

The Chief realized that until the bodies were found or Janaina and Bento turned up there was little that could be done.

Alex and Matt both admitted to each other that both of them had crossed the personal involvement line and that their trip to her parent's place would seal their desire to adopt Aurea. Both of them were finding it hard to wait the couple of days before the trip.

Unconsciously Aurea's curiosity about Alex's parents and where she had grown up provided the conversation that let Alex explain her younger years in a natural way. She shared the fact that she had gone out fishing with her father almost every weekend during the summer.

She had learned to cook and sew from her mother.

She shared the fact that in high school she had been an editor on the school newspaper, had been a cheer leader on the football team and had been elected student council president. Each of those points caused Aurea to ask a bunch of questions and the evenings were full of discussion.

Those discussions led Aurea to ask questions about Matt's early years and how he had met Alex. He said that he had grown up in Mississippi in a small town where his parents raised him and his brothers and sisters. He shared that his family had been very poor. He let her know that he had done very well as a football player. Football had gotten him a chance to become a marine and he had gone to the Navel Academy, graduated, and had then gone to Iraq where he was a sniper.

Aurea asked what a sniper did. He explained the concept but did not explain that he had earned several metals for his actions. Actions that had killed the enemy by shooting them at a very long range.

Aurea sat thinking about both Alex and Matt. She hoped that someday she could be as successful as the two of them seemed to be.

Abandoned

The day before the trip Alex walked from the office over to Aurea's school, let the principal know about the situation in trying to locate Aurea's missing parents and that Aurea would be missing school the rest of the week but if she could get her assignments, she would make sure that Aurea did her homework and not fall behind.

She was pleased that all the teachers involved gave her the homework assignments and when they learned that Alex was going to her mother's house and was taking Aurea, they said that seemed to be a good idea. They asked about Aurea's parents and said they understood that the two had been missing for several weeks and that did not seem to be a good sign.

Alex agreed that the situation was not good but said nothing more. She once again pictured vultures circling overhead.

Trey had walked over with her and on the way back he said that everyone in the office was on edge because of the fact that it was clear to them that she was well over the line of personal involvement but that they were all rooting for her.

She replied that she could not help it. She had fallen in love with Aurea. Having been around her for almost two weeks had been more than she could handle and until the case was solved, she was going to be a wreck. She said that she was leaving for the rest of the week to give everyone in the office a break and it would let her introduce Aurea to her parents and get their reaction.

Trey smiled and said that her parents would fall in love with Aurea just like he and Lindsey and everyone that had met her had. He added that now it was only a matter of time.

As they rode their bikes home, Johnnie commented on the fact that the team was rooting for her and hoped that when the case was over Aurea would end up being in the home where she was currently living.

Alex thanked him for the comment and said that this case had exposed a part of herself that she had not known existed.

Johnnie laughed and asked what that might be.

Alex confessed that she had wanted to start a family but had been afraid to get pregnant. She was afraid of being shot and having her baby get killed. She wanted a family but at the same time, she was selfish enough to want to keep doing what she was doing. It was one of the few situations that she had not known how to resolve.

Johnnie nodded and said that he understood the feeling of "dammed if you do and dammed if you don't." He said that had been his feelings the day he had flagged her down in front of the library. He said that the action he took at that time changed his life. He said that the actions she was taking was going to change her life and like his, her the change would be for the better.

Alex looked up from where she was locking the chain on her bike and thanked him for his words of wisdom.

Abandoned

He nodded and said that he was pushing his bike up to his house since he would be starting his ride in the morning from there. He wished her a good trip to see her mother.

That evening Alex gave Aurea a small suitcase to pack her things that she wanted to take for their two-day visit. She helped Aurea decide which outfits to wear and made sure she had her toothbrush and hair brush.

The two of them then went into the master bedroom where she packed her bag. They pushed both bags out to the back door.

Aurea asked why they were going to leave by the back door and Alex explained that the house really sat level to the street behind the house and the taxi would pick them up there.

Alex asked if a pizza sounded like a good choice for dinner.

Aurea said that she would love a pizza especially one that had lots of cheese on it.

The two of them went online and after a few moments they agreed on a large thin crust pizza with extra cheese and everything on it except hot peppers.

Alex said that while they waited, they should go to the third floor and walk through the art gallery together.

They had only got to discuss the paintings that had been done by Annie when the doorbell rang.

Alex followed Aurea down and told her not to open the door. Once she checked that it was pizza being delivered, she opened the door. She had already paid and given a tip, but she handed the delivery person another tip and said that it was for having climbed the stairs. That got a smile from her and a comment about why they would ever have built the house in such a fashion.

Alex carried the pizza into the kitchen and put it on the table where the two of them dug in.

Matt came home a few minutes later and joined them at the table. He was in time to eat almost half the pizza while it was still warm. He commented that it was one of the better pizza's he had eaten lately but he figured they could go to Alex's mother's Pizza shop and enjoy an even better one.

Aurea laughed and said that now she knew that Alex came from a rich family. Her mother owned a Pizza shop, and her father was a professor.

Alex smiled and said that her mother was also a very successful lawyer in the Chicago area and the pizza shop was her hobby. And that yes, she admitted that she was from a very well-to-do family.

When they got to the airport and Alex led the way to the first-class line, Aurea pulled on Matt's hand and smiled and silently mouthed the word, "rich."

Abandoned

Alex went down the escalator and instead of walking to the far terminal she decided that she would ride the tram so that Aurea would get to ride it.

Aurea said that the last time she had ridden on it was when she and her parents had arrived in Cincinnati.

Alex nodded but said nothing. It was a reminder to her that the reason she was going to Evanston was because she thought that Aurea's parents were dead.

She once again envisioned vultures flying in a circle high in the sky.

As she was walking past the shops going to the gate, she realized that Aurea did not have swimsuit. She led the way into one of the shops featuring swimsuits and asked the clerk if she had an appropriate swimsuit for Aurea.

The clerk took the two of them to one of the counters and pulled several styles out.

Alex asked Aurea which one she liked best.

Aurea looked over to where Matt was standing near the doorway and once again mouthed, "rich." She turned back to the counter and pick the one she liked the best. She and Alex went into the booth where she tried it on. She commented that the lady clerk had a good eye for size and said that it fit just fine.

Alex agreed and said that they would buy it and then they needed to hustle to the gate.

When they got on the plane, Alex asked which seat Aurea wanted to sit in and was not surprised that she wanted the window seat. She herself preferred the aisle seat and Matt had the aisle across from her.

The flight was uneventful.

The surprise came when the three of them were met by Harold Zimmerman at the exit of the plane. He said that he and his team was there to personally escort her and the surprise home for a celebration dinner that her mother was throwing.

Alex looked at his smug face and shook her head. She asked how he had found out about her arrival.

He said that he had officially been sent by the Illinois Lieutenant Governor to escort her and he had no idea about anything that was going on.

Aurea boldly asked who he was and why he was escorting Alex.

Harold knelt down shook her hand and said because the Lieutenant Governor of the State of Illinois had heard that she was coming and decided that such a beautiful young lady deserved to be personally met and protected.

Aurea looked up at Matt and asked if everything was OK.

Matt nodded and said that Alex had quite a reputation and was a lifetime Illinois State Marshall of the highest rank and that the Lieutenant Governor was not only her boss but also her god mother.

Aurea nodded and said that she must be really old.

Abandoned

That got a laugh out of Harold who said that he would never repeat those words.

He led them down the outside steps and over to the van and introduced the rest of his team.

He asked if the luggage was in the back of the van. One of his team pointed to where two baggage handlers were looking for the baggage.

Alex took her wallet from her purse and handed some money to him and said to give it to the baggage handlers. She then got in, took a seat, and had Aurea take the one next to her. Matt took the one closest to the door and closed it.

The luggage was loaded in back and they all left the airport.

During the drive to her house, Alex asked who had shared her surprise with Jane. He said that Jane had learned the secret from someone in Cincinnati.

He added that Jane had somehow wrangled invitations to dinner that evening to Alex's mother's house for all of them but had not shared the secret only that it warranted a celebration. Jane was having the event catered by Rodolpho who ran her mother's pizzeria.

Alex laughed and said that the last few trips to Chicago had consistently been surprising events to her and this one seemed to be off on its own trajectory and she just planned to enjoy it.

Aurea had listened to the conversation. She took Matt's hand and asked what the surprise was going to be.

Matt shook his head back and forth and told her that in a few moments she would find out.

The van turned into the lane leading to Alex's parents' home. It stopped when the tunnel-like tree covering framed the house ahead.

Harold had Aurea stand and take a look.

Aurea asked if that was the house Alex had grown up in. She didn't wait for an answer but looked at Matt and once again said, "rich, but really rich."

The van drove up to the circular driveway and parked.

Rose-Anne and Russel came out of the house and walked briskly out to the van.

Harold and his team formed a greeting lane and Alex, Matt and Aurea were guided up the middle.

Harold announced the arrival of the famous Cincinnati detective, her husband, and the most beautiful surprise that he had ever seen, Aurea.

Rose-Anne went straight to Aurea and gave her a hug and said that she was really happy to have her at her house. She then gave Alex a hug and said that she had been repeatedly pleasantly surprised by what was happening on this visit. She said that Jane had refused to say anything about who Alex was bringing with her but that it would be the surprise of her life.

After giving Matt a hug, she took Aurea's hand, said that she was very happy to have her be the surprise and led all of them into the house.

Abandoned

Alex stopped and listened as her mother went through her lengthy description of the two circular staircases leading to the bedrooms on the second floor. Her mother pointed to the circular chandelier hanging above the circular black mahogany stand that featured a vase of fresh white flower. She then pointed into the spacious greeting room, then turned and pointed into a dining area. Alex then followed her mother and Aurea through the tunnel leading to the grand family room with the six-foot-high fireplace that had carvings of a group of dancing partiers in the floor directly in front of it.

Aurea looked at Alex and smiled and mouthed, "really, really, really rich."

Alex took Aurea's hand and said that she was going to show her the room she would have for the next couple of days. She signaled for Matt to follow her. She looked up the stairs and saw that their suitcases had been put at the top level. She went up and asked that they first all go to the room that she and Matt were staying in.

Once there she sat down on the floor with her back to the bed footboard and asked Aurea to sit down with her. She said that she had not expected to be met by Harold and his team nor had she expected her godmother, who was also the Lieutenant Governor to get involved. She had hoped for a quiet way of sharing both bad news and what she hoped was good news.

Aurea put her hand on hers and said that she thought the bad news was about her parents and she did not want to hear it. She had been counting the days and knew that more days the worse it was for her parents.

She had tears in her eyes when she asked about the good news.

Alex wiped the tears away and said that she hoped what she was going to share would be the good news and that was that she and Matt wanted to adopt her.

Aurea smiled and said that would be wonderful and leaned into Alex and gave her a hug. She did the same to Matt who was sitting to her other side.

She then stopped and asked about her grandmother and would she be a problem.

Alex said that she had plans to deal with her so that she would allow the adoption. She then suggested that they all change into poolside clothes and go downstairs and finish the tour by joining the party that would be going on there.

Aurea gave her a hug again and quietly said that Alex had grown up as a rich girl.

Alex nodded and said that she had always been parent rich and had never taken into account that she had also been rich in the other physical things.

Abandoned

Once out by pool side, Alex decided to enjoy the party. She watched as Aurea jumped into the pool and swam back and forth. She took in the conversation and realized that everyone was very much aware of her intension of adopting Aurea and thought it was a really good idea.

Dexter, the owner of the Golden Goose yacht, came over to her and asked if she wanted to go out fishing in the morning.

Alex said that she was indeed looking forward to it but that this time perhaps they should plan on going out at a reasonable hour that was more like eight or nine in the morning.

Dexter nodded and said that time would be fine and that everything would be ready. She should relax and just show up. He smiled and said that he hoped that the adoption would go smoothly.

Ron Mueller

Abandoned

Chapter 5: The Golden Goose

When Jane arrived, she lavished praise on the idea of having Aurea in the family. She was dressed in red and wore a yellow rose near her left shoulder.

Alex thought about a long-ago time at a Christmas party when she was a few years older than Aurea when she had first noticed the looks her aunt drew for the very fashionable way of dressing. She smiled as she thought that Jane had retained all of that beauty.

She was well aware that Jane had been re-elected twice because not only did she do a superb job, but she also knew how to work the press and the public. She worked the celebration party and had everyone supporting a new family member.

It turned out that everyone that was at dinner was also planning to go out fishing on the Golden Goose.

The celebration went well into the evening and Alex was exhausted by the time they went up to bed. She was glad that she had arranged for a late start to the fishing trip.

Alex knew that Dexter would not accept payment for the outing but as always, she would gift his favorite charity with the amount that he charged to rent the yacht. This was a quietly agreed-to-way that they had settled on when she had insisted that she pay for using the yacht. He still blamed himself because he had rented a fishing boat to an old college friend who then attacked and wounded Alex because of her skin color. After that he had declared that she could go out on the Golden Goose free whenever she wanted.

She could not accept that arrangement and finally settled on gifting one of his favorite charities.

In the morning after a leisurely early morning breakfast, Alex led the way into the garage and over to her shining black Jaguar. As always, her father had gotten it detailed as well as having its maintenance done before her arrival. She put the top down and asked Aurea to sit in the back and enjoy the ride to the fishing pier where the boat they were going out on was docked.

Aurea looked at the car and asked whose it was.

Alex said that it was hers. She said that her father had given it to her as a high school graduation gift. It was an old car when he had given it to her and said that now she could register it as an antique. She had kept it at home because until she had bought the house in Cincinnati, she had no place to park it.

Abandoned

Aurea walked around the car with her hands on it and said that she didn't want to say anything, but she did not know anyone who had received such a beautiful gift for a high school graduation.

The ride to the boat dock took only a few minutes and they were quiet minutes where the only sound was that of Aurea humming.

When Aurea saw the Golden Goose, she asked if that was the ship they were going to fish from and was that the one that Alex's father had taken her fishing on.

Alex pointed to where her father's boat that was tied to the pier and said that was the boat they had used.

Aurea nodded and said that made her feel better.

When everyone got on board, they all headed out to the spot where almost every weekend, when she was Aurea's age and to the present time, she and her father fished. She watched as this time her father helped Aurea bait her line and then taught her how to cast it out.

Her mother quietly asked how she felt.

Alex smiled and said that watching Aurea with her father brought back many happy memories and now the memories would have a new twist.

She asked her mother whether she would work up the adoption papers, select the court and judge to adjudicate it.

Her mother nodded and said that she would do it and treat it as one of her gratis cases.

That got a chuckle from Alex who said that she would be glad to pay her outrageous fees. She got a hug and heard her mother say that she was so happy that Alex was adopting Aurea.

They both looked over where Aurea was laughing as she pulled in a large lake trout. She was getting coaching from about four different people, but Alex's father was the one that was giving the helping hand and making sure that Aurea was letting the trout run but was slowly getting her to bring it in toward the boat.

Rodolfo came over and said that his boss had informed him that she wanted to have a special pizza for lunch the following day.

Alex said that she wanted him to surprise her and serve whatever pizza he thought would be the most interesting one he could think of, but she knew that Aurea liked extra cheese

He nodded and said that he was going to think very hard on that order. He then asked how many people were going to have lunch with her. She looked around and said that there would most likely only be five people in total.

He said that he would prepare two special pizzas.

Alex looked over to where her father was holding a large multi-speckled trout that was about two thirds as long as Aurea was tall. She rushed over and took several pictures. She then asked what Aurea wanted to do with the trout.

Aurea looked at it and asked if she could get it mounted and hung up in their family room back in Cincinnati.

Abandoned

Alex nodded and then heard Dexter say that he would arrange to get it done.

Aurea then asked if she could fish some more.

Matt said that she could but only if he got to help her this time.

Alex chose to stand on one side of Aurea while Matt helped her bait the line and then stepped away to let her cast it. The cast was not as far as Alex's father had cast the previous line, but it must have been to the right spot because almost immediately she had a strike and was fighting yet another fish. This time the trout was almost as large as the previous one, but it proved to be tougher to bring in. By the time she had it next to the boat and Matt had it in the scoop net it was clear that she was worn out.

Rose-Anne said that she would serve that trout for dinner that evening along with baked vegetables.

Alex led the way to where Dexter was grilling hamburgers, bratwurst, and sausages.

Aurea pointed to a hamburger and said that she wanted it on a bun with a tomato slice and lettuce.

Alex prepared the burger and asked what condiments Aurea wanted.

The choice was ketchup, and mayonnaise but no mustard.

They all sat down at the table under the canopy and sipped on their lemonade. Alex had chosen a bratwurst and Matt had a hamburger with everything on it.

The fishing seemed to naturally taper off as everyone chose to have something to eat.

Alex saw Dexter cleaning the second trout that Aurea had caught and realized that she would not need to do it. She was already looking forward to how her Chef Mother would prepare it. She knew that it would be some wonderful creation that would taste like no other trout before it. She was sure her mother was already thinking through how to make the dinner special. The loving way that both her mother and father were treating Aurea made her realize how much she had counted on their support and acceptance. She was now reassured that her own deep feelings about the situation had the support of the people she counted on most.

Dexter made sure everyone had their fishing lines in and were ready to go back to shore. He then guided the Golden Goose back to the pier and displayed his ability by the way he brought in and tied it off himself.

As they walked up the pier, Alex heard Aurea ask her father whether they could go out in his boat to go fishing. Her father nodded and asked if she wanted to go out early the following morning. Alex smiled and wondered if she should go along. She then heard Matt ask if he could go along. Alex decided that she should be a chauffeur but let her father and Matt go with Aurea.

Abandoned

Rose-Anne wondered how Alex was taking the attention that Aurea was getting from everyone. It was clear to her that Alex had transitioned into a loving mother. She hoped that the adoption would work out otherwise she knew Alex's heart would be broken.

She planned to have the paperwork ready before the three of them left.

The afternoon was spent by the pool where everyone relaxed, chatted, and watched as Aurea enjoyed the pool, just floating and paddling around from the sunny side of the pool to that part that was in the shade.

Rose-Anne decided that making the dinner special would entail her getting Aurea to help prepare it. She asked Aurea if she wanted to help her prepare Trout Almondine for dinner.

Alex smiled as Aurea said that she would love to. She decided to watch to see how Aurea would take to helping get everything prepared.

Her mother led the way into her kitchen where she put on her chef's toque and adjusted one and put it on Aurea's head. She then put on her apron and found a smaller one for Aurea. She had some small plastic gloves that were still too large for Aurea but would serve the purpose.

She then placed three trout on a cutting board and said that she was going to prepare two of them and that Aurea would prepare the one she caught..

Ron Mueller

Alex was using her phone to record each step of preparing the Trout Almondine.

Her mother steaked two of the trout and helped Aurea steak her trout.

She took time to show Aurea how to hold the knife and curl the finger tips of the hand holding the fish. She joked about the fact that finger tips would ruin the Almondine.

Then her mother chopped most of the onions but showed Aurea how to cut the onion in half and put the flat side down before slicing it and then chopping it.

She then had her chop a few of the onions.

She then salted and peppered the steaked fish on both sides.

The next step was to brown some almond flakes in a skillet and after removing the almonds from the frying pan, she put some olive oil in and let it get hot while she began to coat the steaked trout with flour.

Rose-Anne was going slow on purpose so that Aurea could keep up.

When the oil in the frying pan was, she carefully placed the trout skin down to get the presentation side a nice brown color. She explained this to Aurea and let her put a couple of slices of trout into the pan.

Aurea was engrossed by getting to do what Rose-Anne was showing her.

While the trout was browning, some potatoes and asparagus was prepared and put into the oven.

Abandoned

She then poured a glass of sherry into the frying pan and got the pan to flambe. The fire in the frying pan was a highlight of the preparation and a surprise to Aurea. As the flambe ended the fish were place on a serving tray. Rose-Anne added some chopped onions and a cup of heavy cream into the frying pan and then she pinched in some salt and sprinkled black pepper over the contents of the large frying pan. She continued to have Aurea repeat each of her steps.

The final step was to chop some chives and mixed it with the sauce that remained after the fish were removed from the frying. She stirred it and added some more butter.

Then it was time to put the sauce over the fish that had been neatly arranged on the serving dish. The final step was to sprinkle on the roasted almonds and put two stems of chive across each fish steak.

Aurea was all smiles as she put on the chive on the fish.

The baked potatoes and asparagus were also ready and put on serving dishes.

Together they split the baked potatoes, put butter, chopped chives in the split, and put each potato in a separate dish. They put butter on the hot asparagus and put the asparagus and potatoes on the separate serving dishes.

Rose-Anne declared the dinner ready and said that they had to quickly set the dinner table out by the pool.

Once that was done, she and Aurea carried out the food and called everyone to dinner.

Everyone commented about the great dinner and how good the Trout Almondine tasted.

Aurea said that it was the first time she had been allowed to cook and she thought it was better than fishing.

Alex smiled and said that she had enjoyed watching much more than fishing as well.

That evening she let her father know that she was going fishing with him as well. She did not plan to fish but she was going to go to take pictures of the fishing trip.

Her father said that he was glad she had decided to go along. He was sure they would all have a great time.

Her mother said that she had some things to do and she would look forward to again having Aurea cook the evening dinner with her.

Abandoned

Chapter 6: Fishing and Pizza

Alex and Aurea sat in back and Matt and her father were in front of the Jag as they drove in the early morning dark to the docks. Once they arrived, Matt and her father went to get the boat ready, and she and Aurea walked up to the bait shop to get the bait. The shop was very interesting to Aurea who looked at the variety of bait that was available.

She made the comment that the bait section smelled funny.

Dexter enjoyed showing the variety of bait that he had on hand and said that Aurea should try each kind to see which was the best bait. He said that somedays one type was better than another, but he had no clue what would work the best that day, so he said he was sending Aurea fishing with a little of each.

Aurea said that the only ones that bothered her were the wiggly grubs and the crickets. She thought the grubs were gross and she felt sorry for the crickets. She said the worms didn't bother her, but they were so big that they would be hard to put on the hook.

Dexter laughed and showed her a handful of smaller worms and put them in a box and gave them to her as well. When he offered her some minnows Aurea said that she couldn't have them put on the hook.

Alex led the way to the boat. It was still the moment in the morning when the sky was slowly going from a black to an early morning grey just before the sun finally won the battle and the sky went to a cloud covered light blue.

Once they were all in and underway out in the lake, her father asked Aurea if she would like to guide the boat.

She knelt on the seat and put her hands on the steering wheel.

Alex took pictures of her father standing behind Aurea ready to take over if necessary.

Once they got to their fishing spot and the engine was off. The poles were prepared, and her father cast the line in for Aurea.

Alex sat on the edge of the boat taking pictures. Aurea was in the front seat and Matt was fishing from the side. Her father was up with Aurea helping her, but he was soon back with her as he let Aurea fish on her own.

Aurea and Matt were both having good luck and it was not too long before they each had a couple. Aurea challenged Matt to a contest to see who would catch the most fish.

Alex watched as Aurea tried each of the bait. It turned out that the gross grubs were what the fish were biting on and soon Aurea was well into the lead with a large number of crappies, two trout and one bass.

Abandoned

It was clear that she was enjoying the crappies because they were biting, and they were easy for her to pull in. She seemed to pull in one after another in a steady stream.

Her father was cleaning them as she pulled them in and then he put them on ice. He commented that he would rather clean them while they were out on the lake then get back and have to stand at the cleaning station.

Matt said that he surrendered and put his pole away and cleaned the fish he had caught. He had chosen to focus on the bass and trout rather than the crappies.

Aurea finally said she was done and that she thought it was more fun to fish from the smaller boat.

Alex said she agreed and that she was glad that Aurea had caught enough for their dinner that evening.

Aurea smiled and said that she hoped she would be able to help prepare dinner that night.

They got back to the pier just before lunch.

Alex made a call to her mother and suggested they meet at the pizza shop.

Rodolpho greeted them and said that he would put the pizzas into the oven and then led them to a table that he had prepared. He pointed to the variety of drinks and said they should help themselves to whatever they might want.

Alex settled for iced tea. She looked around and noted that most of the tables were full. She was happy to see that her mother's Pizzeria was doing well.

Rodolpho had three pizzas brought to the table. He pointed to one that he said was a thin crust tavern style Chicago pizza with extra cheese and peperoni. The second one was a New York style made with a hand tossed thin crust and the third one was a West Coast pizza made the way the Caltech college students liked it. He smiled and said that he had chosen to make the three so that Aurea could get a taste of pizza across the country, but ones that were made in the best Pizzeria in the world.

Alex cut three smaller pieces and put it on one of the plates and handed it to Aurea. She then put the same size pieces on her plate before getting out of the way as everyone took a piece.

They were all chatting and enjoying lunch when a young woman excused herself and asked if she could get Alex's autograph.

Alex was surprised as she listened to the young lady explain that she was going to North Western because she had learned that was where Alex had gone. She said that she had read about her saving the young girl that had been missing for fifteen years. She was also aware of the coal barge she had sunk as she battled mafia hit men out in Lake Michigan.

Alex was a little taken aback but she nodded and said that she did not have a pen.

The young woman handed her a pen and a book by Professor Raymond Szymanski, "How to Profile a Killer."

Abandoned

Alex recognized the name of her favorite professor. He had taught her and the entire Cincinnati detective department using that book. She knew that the young lady was indeed influenced by her own academic career. She wrote, "Hope you do well, and I look forward to your success," and signed it.

She watched the young lady go back to where she was sitting with a young man. She looked over to her mother and said that she was a little surprised, but she figured that her admirer had come to the Pizzeria hoping to get that signature.

Aurea had listened to the exchange. She looked at Matt and said, "very rich and very famous."

After enjoying the pizza and complementing Rodolpho on the great pizza, they all returned to the house and went out by the pool and relaxed.

Alex sat reading and watched as Aurea swam or lay on a towel in the sun. She dozed off and when she awoke, she learned that Aurea was in the kitchen making a strawberry rhubarb pie and getting the crappies ready to be fried for dinner. She went into the kitchen in time to see Aurea putting the crisscross strips on the top of the pie. She then watched as her mother showed how to prepare the crappies with some salt and pepper seasoning. Her father had removed the scales but left the heads on in the style that her mother preferred.

Aurea asked about what would go best with the fish.

Alex listened as her mother suggested they have fresh mashed potatoes topped with butter and a serving of grilled cauliflower on the main plates and have a sliced tomato and olive oil salad on the side. Her mother made the point that the dinner would be simple but delicious and desert would be warm rhubarb pie with a scoop of vanilla ice cream.

Alex smiled as Aurea said that she couldn't wait until she tried the rhubarb pie because desert was always what she based how good a dinner had been. She added that she had never tasted rhubarb pie.

Alex had been reading the adoption papers her mother had given her when she dosed off sitting out by the pool. She knew this was a sign that Aurea had been accepted into the family. It was clear that she had made the right choice in coming home to get the slow case's slow progress out of her mind. She dreaded returning to Cincinnati because she had talked to Johnnie and knew that no progress had been made.

Friday morning after breakfast, she drove the Jag to the airport. He father was along to take the Jag back home. They all hugged at the curb before the three of them went over to the check in counter.

The flight was short and uneventful. She saw that Matt was taking the opportunity to take a nap. Once back in Cincinnati they all got into the car and drove home.

Abandoned

Aurea had been quiet on the way home. When she got to the house she asked if her mom and dad had been found. She had tears in her eyes.

Alex felt a pang of sadness go through her. She had been so focused on her own feelings that she felt guilty about forgetting about Aurea's feelings. She gave her a hug and said that she would immediately let her know when she learned anything about her mom and dad. She knelt down and gave Aurea a hug.

Aurea nodded and said that she was expecting bad news, but she still wanted to know what had happened.

Alex said that she expected bad news too, but she wanted Aurea to know that she was loved and would always have a place with her and Matt.

Aurea nodded and added that she also now had a grandmother that would teach her how to cook and a grandfather that she could go fishing with.

Matt acted hurt and asked why she didn't want to go fishing with him.

That seemed to break the spell and Aurea laughed and said that they should go fishing every weekend.

Matt said that he knew a lake where they could go on the weekend. He then excused himself and said that he had to get ready to get to work.

Ron Mueller

There was a knock on the back door and Johnnie and Mary came in carrying a large casserole dish and a bowel with a mixed salad. They said that they had brought over a dinner offering and hoped that they could all figure out what to do on a Friday evening. They suggested finding a good old-fashioned movie and just chilling out on the couch.

While Mary and Aurea got the table set, Johnnie let Alex know that no progress had been made in locating Aurea's parents. He said that he had been able to get all the information needed for the Brazilian arrest. He added that he had all the firewalls hacked and the ability to get a video feed from the bar that Christiano used as his headquarters. He then said that he had checked with the forest service officer and had his assurance that his team was watching the sky as they had been asked to.

Alex knew that it would be a long weekend for her. She decided to take a long bike ride with Aurea on Saturday morning and on Sunday afternoon Matt could take her fishing. The rest of the time would be spent out in the back yard or making sure that Aurea was ready to go back to school with all her homework done.

The weekend seemed to drag by. Alex was glad that Matt had offered to take Aurea fishing. They drove to Caesar Creek State Park where they rented a boat and went out fishing. The fishing was OK but nothing like what they had experienced out on Lake Michigan. They stopped fishing after catching several nice sized crappies.

Abandoned

Alex stopped at the cleaning station and gutted the fish while Matt drove with Aurea and found a table located under a covered area. He returned and picked her up and they set up the picnic table with the chicken, onion rings and cold slaw lunch they had picked up on the way.

It was good that they had chosen a table that was under roof because not long after they had started to eat the rain began and it was heavy enough that they could not see the lake. They were enjoying lunch, just chatting with each other, and watching the rain come down in buckets.

Aurea commented that the rain reminded her of the rain back in Brazil where she was allowed to run out in the rain and get totally soak. She smiled and said that it was like swimming, but she could walk, look up and open her mouth and take the water in.

Alex said that she could run out in the rain if she wanted to.

Aurea shook her head and said that the rain seemed to be too cold to have fun in it.

Alex agreed and said that she liked the sound of the rain hitting the roof while they were all able to stay dry. By the time they got done with what she thought of as their picnic dinner the rain had subsided, and she suggested they drive back home and, on the way, stop at their favorite ice cream shop and enjoy desert there before going home and getting ready for Monday.

Ron Mueller

Abandoned

<u>Chapter 7: The Circling Vultures</u>

Alex and Johnnie rode in to work and Mary took Aurea to school. Alex had made sure that Aurea had all her homework done and had reviewed it. She was very pleased with Aurea's neat writing and how she clearly organized her homework. She had also made sure that Aurea was wearing one of her new outfits.

On her ride into the station, she was thinking on how she could somehow break the barrier that she faced in closing the case.

Johnnie could tell that Alex was focused on thinking about the case, so he purposely asked questions about her trip home and about how the fishing had been. He knew that they were currently depending on vultures to give all of them a break in the case. That worried him. He hoped he was right about the vultures supper sensitive smelling ability.

She and Johnnie were the first to arrive. Alex got herself a cup of coffee before going to her desk. They were usually the first and this morning it gave Alex a moment to think about how she needed to conduct herself. She knew that she had so far her personal behavior caused the team to be on edge.

She was having trouble figuring out what to do to break the case. She was anxious to make things happen but had no clue how she could make that happen. She knew she had to tone down her current behavior.

Trevor was getting on her nerve with his constant joking about the rate at which she was making progress, but she had to handle it better than she had done so far.

Johnnie had made significant progress in the information he was accumulating on Christiano that would make it easy to nail him if any bodies were ever found.

He had also done a complete work up on Aurea's grandmother who was now a widow for about a year. She was surviving on a pittance of a government allowance. He said that it was harder to get specifics about her day-to-day life because she was not on the internet or any social media, but he had found her address.

Alex figured that the grandmother would be open to allowing her granddaughter to be adopted if there was something in it for her.

Abandoned

She contacted the Brazilian consulate and got the adoption paperwork required by the Brazilian government. She visited the consulates office and got help in properly filling it out. Her goal was to make sure that it was exactly what the Brazilian government required. When she was done, she knew that all that she would need would be the grandmother's signature and the signature of witness to that signature to make it official.

She planned to seek the signature by explaining the situation and she was prepared to offer the grandmother an income that would match the average income in Brazil in exchange for her signature on the adoption papers. She had already decided that she would feel better if the grandmother had the income, so she asked Johnnie to locate the nearest bank and to set up an account in the grandmother's name and put in seven thousand dollars.

She figured that having the account in place would make sure that she would walk out with the adoption paperwork signed.

A few moments after she sat down at her desk, Trey came in with his cup of coffee and asked how her trip home had gone.

Alex was about to share the highlights of the trip when Bill and Trevor walked in.

Trevor held out the box of donuts and said that salvation was on hand.

As he did on almost every morning, Trey took out a bear claw, broke it in half, and gave half to Alex.

Ron Mueller

She took a bite and a sip of coffee then said that she wanted to apologize for having driven the team to the edge and she wanted to thank whoever had leaked her desire to adopt Aurea to the Illinois Lieutenant Governor because that person had done her a great favor.

She added that she was going to do her best to stop driving them crazy.

Trevor looked at Bill and asked if he had made such a call.

Bill shook his head and said that Trevor knew full well that neither of them had done such a thing because the two of them had enjoyed their fishing trip to Lake Cumberland and having a picnic with their wives.

The Chief had come over for a donut and said that he had not called Jane or even talked to her for several months.

Johnnie shook his head and said that he was innocent.

Trey looked at Alex raised his hand and said that Lindsey had her back and insisted that he make the call. He had explained the situation in detail to Jane. She had let him know that she knew exactly how to handle the situation.

Alex went over to Trey and gave him a hug and thanked him. She then said that it was just what she had needed.

She then said that Aurea had a great time and she finally recognized how deeply she had gotten into this case. Never before had she let herself let it be so personal but this time she could not control her feelings.

Abandoned

She added that she was still overwhelmed by her feelings, but her mother helped put everything into perspective. She pointed out that the situation seemed to point to the fact that Aurea was already an orphan. Also watching Aurea have a great time allowed her to accept the fact that her feelings were the right ones.

She then stopped talking and asked if there was anything new and took another sip of coffee as she watched everyone shake their heads in the negative.

The Chief told everyone to take it easy and perhaps go to the gun range and practice. He said that it always worked for him to go there to reduce his stress.

Alex said that she was going to take his advice. She was greeted by the range master who asked her if she wanted a blindfold to see if she could duplicate her previous achievement of shooting out the bullseye while blindfolded.

Alex smiled, shook her head, and replied that she wanted to relish repeatedly seeing the bullseye disappear and added that she wanted her gun barrel to turn red from repeat firing.

The range master asked what had her so worked up.

Trey was standing at the next firing station preparing to practice as well. He said that he should just watch Alex shoot and not get her started on what was bothering her.

Alex nodded and put on her hearing protection and then checked her weapon before raising it and firing.

She turned, sent out her target and began firing.

Ron Mueller

Trey stopped after he had used three targets and watched as Alex repeatedly pulled in her target and put out another one. She went through half a dozen targets as she played with putting patterns in them as well as shooting out the bullseye. She shot her initials into the last target, pulled it in and put down her gun. Its barrel was not red hot, and she had gone through a box of bullets.

The range master picked up her used targets and laughed and said that he would see if he could give her a master marksman rating. He added that he hoped she would be able to solve whatever case she was on otherwise he would need to order extra ammunition for her to use.

This caused Alex to smile and say that she was sure that there would be no other case that would affect her the same way as the one that the team was currently facing.

She and Trey were standing at the cleaning station and cleaning their weapons when she said that she was ready to go searching through all the forests in Ohio to find the graves of Aurea's parents. She looked at him and asked if he thought they were dead or if they were in hiding.

Trey simply replied, "dead." He then said that it was time to get back to their desks and have another cup of coffee. He added that his practice had helped him and then watching her he realized how the case was affecting her.

When they got back to their desks, Johnnie suggested they walk to their favorite Thai restaurant and have lunch.

Abandoned

Everyone agreed that would be a great idea.

Once they were seated in the restaurant and had their orders in Alex made a point of asking Bill and Trevor how the fishing at Lake Cumberland had gone.

Trevor went into a long description of having to constantly duck as Bill cast his line and having to help Bill get his fish into the boat. His tale had everyone at the table chuckling and Bill defending himself.

Alex knew well enough that Trevor was doing his best to lighten the moment. He was a relentless teaser, but he was also a great fearless detective. He and Bill made a great pair.

They were just getting ready to leave when Alex's phone buzzed with the sound she had assigned to the Forest Service. She put up her hand, put her phone into speaker mode, put it on the table and everyone leaned in to listen. The ranger said that he had thought watching vultures was a crazy idea, then after a pause he added that it had worked and that he was standing at the site where they had found what seemed to be a grave.

He added that his team would never be able to see buzzards circling without going to check out what they were circling over.

He had called her as soon as it had been found and wondered what he should do next.

Everyone at the table all said, "finally," at the same time.

Alex asked him to block the area off and to keep his folks from wandering around because she wanted it treated like a crime scene. She would arrange for the coroner and his team to come out to the site and take over its management and dig up the graves. She then asked if he could give her the directions to the site.

He chuckled and said that his map addict on the team had written down the coordinates and he was texting them to her as they spoke.

She said that she wanted to reward his group not only with public recognition but also with a personal reward from her if the find turned out to be the graves of the two she was looking for.

The service officer was silent for a moment and then said that there was only one grave.

That gave Alex pause. She looked around the table to see the reaction. She was less sure about what had been found but she still planned to ask Dr. Rogers to take his team out and dig up the grave.

Trevor commented that they had the experience of finding two bodies in one grave and he was putting his bet on the fact that they would find two in that single grave.

She hung up and let Trey know that she was going to the morgue to get Dr. Rogers out to the site.

Trevor shook his head and laughed. He commented that now he would have to tell his friends that his team was using vultures to solve murder cases.

Abandoned

Alex nodded and replied that it was better than relying on him to give her a clue on what to do.

Bill laughed and added that except for Johnnie the rest of the team had been clueless from the start, and he was for giving Johnnie the choice of where to have the celebration and it would be on Trevor's dime.

Trevor did a little bow to Johnnie and complemented him on not only being Alex's magician but also a vulture whisper.

When she entered the lab, Dr. Rogers looked up from his desk and commented that if she was coming to the lab without him calling her it meant that she was going to ask him and his team to do something out of the ordinary and that probably meant extra work. He then asked what was up?

Alex explained the situation and asked him to take his team to the coordinates that had been given her by a forest ranger that had found a grave that might hold two bodies.

Dr. Rogers smiled and said that last time he and his team had gone out for her they had ended up processing more than sixteen bodies and going through an eight towered ten thousand square foot house looking for finger prints and bullets. He hoped that this time it would indeed be only two bodies.

Alex let him know that she was going to let the Chief know about what she was sure was a break in the case and she wanted to follow him to the location where the ranger was waiting for them.

Alex left the morgue and went up and informed the Chief. She knew that she had also stressed him when he commented that he hope this would let her close the case.

She and Trey walked out to their old police car, and she asked him to drive so she could make some calls.

Trey followed the van used by Dr. Rogers.

Dr. Rogers knew that this case seemed to be very personal for Alex and that solving it held some other implications that he was not aware of. He would tread lightly as he processed the bodies until he understood the situation.

He had his GPS coordinates set to the one given him by the forest service officer and was driving carefully through the country roads leading to the site. He realized that there were two cars following him and wondered who else was following.

His arrival was greeted by at least half a dozen forest rangers standing in front of a taped in area of the forest. He was glad that he had been using GPS because he would otherwise never have found the site.

He arranged to have his van driven near the grave site but asked that everyone stand back in case he found any footprints or tire tracks.

The ranger said that his team might have made many of the footprints when they were looking for the grave, but they had not driven any vehicles into the area.

The ranger walked with him to the spot where they thought was the grave.

Abandoned

Dr. Rogers had his team set everything up and he had one of them using a ground radar at the grave site so that they would have visual confirmation before removing the stones over the suspected grave. He wanted an initial scan, so his team had an estimate of the depth to the body.

The radar image showed more than two feet so he was sure that there would be two bodies and had his team prepare two carrying boards.

Alex stood back with the rest of the team. She asked why Bill and Trevor had come along.

Trevor laughed and said that the Chief had told them to have Trey's back in case they had to engage in any gun battles in the forest.

Bill shoulder bumped Trevor and made the point that the Chief had said nothing of the sort but the two of them were bored and figured that going on a drive to witness what the vultures had found was more interesting than sitting at their desks twiddling their fingers.

She pointed to where Dr. Rogers team was digging and said that she figured that it was indeed a grave.

Alex said that the four of them should examine the area around the grave to see if they could come up with any evidence that might be useful.

Trey pointed to several boot prints and put-up evidence markers. He went over to where the rangers were standing and verified that none of them had a similar looking boot heal.

Trevor and Bill said they would make a sweep between the trees near the grave. Bill picked up a thin flat rock and let out a whistle and pointed under the rock.

Trevor held out an evidence bag as Bill put on his gloves and lifted the rock to show a revolver with a silencer laying under the rock. He was about to pick it up, but Alex asked him to wait so that Dr. Rogers camera person could film the find.

Dr. Rogers walked over and looked at the revolver. He commented that he would take the gun in with the bodies that were being dug up and get the lab to process it for fingerprints and to match it to the bullets that he now figured he would find in the cadavers.

His team was lifting out the first body they had just dug up and getting it ready for transport. Alex saw that they had a second board ready for another body and felt fairly certain that Aurea's parents had been found. She asked if the first body was that of a woman.

Dr. Rogers put up his hand and said that everyone, but his team should stay back. He walked over to where the first body was strapped to a board and verified that it was a woman. He looked at Alex and said that it was very likely that they had found the husband and wife that she was looking for.

Alex said they should look for additional boot prints that matched the one found by Trey.

Abandoned

As the four of them worked their way closer to the grave they found several more boot prints. She had Trey get a plaster mix from their crime scene case.

He cast the boot prints that they found. The casts revealed that the heel on the right boot had a distinctive zig zag crack in it.

She took pictures of the casts and then turned them over to Dr. Rogers' team.

The second body was lifted out and prepared for transport.

Dr. Rogers verified that it was a male and said that he and the team would return to the station and do the detailed autopsy there.

Alex asked the rangers to keep the crime scene tape up and leave the grave open. She would let them know when everything could be turned back over to nature.

Johnnie had launched Gunjfor and was standing with the entire ranger unit. He was flying Gunjfor in a circle with the vultures and giving them a view from up high.

They were all laughing and saying that they now had a much better understanding of how lucky they all were to have vultures in the sky.

Alex, Trey, Bill, and Trevor all walked over and again complemented Johnnie on the fact that he had provided the means of cracking the case.

On the drive back to the station, Trey asked what she was planning to do about Aurea. She looked over at him and said that she was going to verify that Aurea wanted to live with her and Matt. She was hoping that would be the case.

He nodded and asked what Matt thought about her idea.

She said she would not have ever let her intentions leak the adoption idea with him if Matt had not already agreed to it.

Trey then asked if Aurea had any other family members that might be interested in raising her.

Alex let him know about the grandmother on the husband's side.

He then asked about the complications that might arise in working with the Brazilian government on her adoption.

Alex said that she had already gotten all the paperwork processed and now she planned to go to Brazil to get everything officially settled.

Trey looked over to her and said that he was looking forward to backing her up in Brazil.

She asked why he thought he would be going.

He looked at her and asked why she thought he wasn't going.

They arrived at the station and after parking the car they walked in together.

The Chief called them into his office and asked them to bring him up to date. He let them know that he had followed all the radio exchange that had occurred, but he wanted to get their perspective.

Abandoned

Alex recounted what Dr. Rogers and his team had found and what she, Trey, Bill, and Trevor had found. She shared that Dr. Rogers, and his team had the bodies down in the morgue and were doing autopsies.

He asked her how she planned to close the case and what she was planning to do about Aurea when she closed the case.

Alex said that she was planning to charge Christiano with murder and was going to adopt Aurea.

The Chief apologized about laughing and said that once again she was able to surprise him. He asked how she was going reach into Brazil and arrest Christiano.

Alex shook her head and said that at the moment she was not sure, but she was planning to go to Brazil and before she left to go there, she would let him know.

He then asked about how she planned to adopt Aurea.

She reached into her purse and lifted out a folder and put it on his desk.

The Chief opened it and slowly leafed through the several pages in the folder. He said that they looked official, but they were in a language that he could not read.

Alex said that they were the adoption papers that she was going to get Aurea's grandmother to sign.

The Chief looked at her and said that he hoped she would be gentle with the grandmother.

Alex nodded and said that she would be kind, sympathetic, and generous but that she intended on leaving Brazil with a successful agreement to the adoption.

The Chief looked at Trey and said that if Alex had any intention of confronting Christiano, he wanted him to have her back. That meant that if there was any evidence that linked Christiano with the murders, Alex was not to go alone to Brazil.

Trey looked at Alex, then back to the Chief, nodded and said that he would have her back. She would not make the trip to Brazil alone. He would be with her even if he had to travel on his own dime.

The Chief shook his head and said that he was officially on the case and normal expenses would be paid by the department.

The Chief's phone rang. He put it on speaker mode, and they heard Dr. Rogers say that he was ready for the preliminary report, and they should come down to the morgue.

The Chief led the way out of his office. He called over to Bill, Trevor and Johnnie and said they should follow.

Dr. Rogers greeted them and pointed to the two bodies that were covered by white sheets. He said that they were both in their late twenties. The woman was white, and the male was brown and most likely of mixed parents. He said that he had run their DNA against the DNA that he had from some hair samples that Alex had provided. He added that there was a parental match.

Abandoned

He added that the two had been shot at close range and it appeared to him that the two might have tried to overcome their killer because of the way they were shot. He said that the gruesome part was that the ears of the male were cut off and his tongue seemed to have been ripped out. He said that his team might need to go back to the grave to see if they could find them.

There was a moment of silence, then Johnnie spoke up and said that he knew where the body parts could be found.

He asked to use Dr. Rogers' computer, sat down and a few moments later he was able to project a view of Cristiano pointing to a placard that had a tongue and two ears mounted on it with the words, "Here is what happens to those who try to leave our team," but the words were in Portuguese. Johnnie said that he had been able to get through the rather poor computer fire wall and get into the camera system used by the bar where the placard was hanging. He added that he had the address of the bar as well.

Dr. Rogers asked how Alex wanted him to proceed.

Alex asked him to finish doing a thorough autopsy. She would work with the Brazilian Consulate to have his work documented, authenticated and the information sent to the Sao Paulo Senior Delegado which she explained was the long name for Chief of Police.

She planned to go to Brazil retrieve the tongue and ears and have their DNA run to verify they belonged to Bento Carvalho that was currently laying on his embalming table. She hoped to also be able to find the boots that had been at the grave site and turn all the evidence all over to their counter parts in Brazil and have Christiano charged for murder.

She looked over to Trey and asked if he would take a picture of Bento with his missing ears and missing tongue.

Dr. Rogers shook his head and had one of his team take the pictures and send them to the team. He said that he was trying to keep the autopsy as uncontaminated as possible. He still had a few steps to get it all done and wanted to keep everyone away.

The Chief thanked Dr. Rogers and asked to be informed when the autopsy was complete. He then led the way back to his office. He looked around at everyone and commented that once again the team had unraveled a complex case, and it was getting a unique ending. He asked what Alex wanted to get out to the news.

Alex said that she had promised the Forest Ranger Chief a spotlight but that she wanted any news announcement to be held after she had Cristiano arrested.

She looked over at Trey and asked if he was willing to fly to Sao Paulo on the following day.

Trey nodded and said that he would need a visa stamp on his passport to be able get into the country.

Abandoned

Alex nodded added that she too needed a visa and said that she was sure they could get them from the Brazilian Consulate, especially if the Chief gave him a call and explained the situation.

She had extra energy when later she and Johnnie rode their bikes across downtown. They rode until the slope up the hill got to the point where it was easier to walk than to bike.

Johnnie asked if she had any idea of how Aurea was going to take the news of her parents death.

Alex shook her head negatively. She said that the hardest part of the day was still ahead of her. She was not sure how she should break the news.

Johnnie suggested that she let Mary deliver the really bad news and that she be the one that offered to have Aurea live with her.

Alex continued pushing her bike up the walkway and thought about Johnnie's suggestion. She was chaining her bike to the bike rack in front of her house when she finally answered him.

She asked if he thought Mary would be willing to do what he suggested.

Johnnie smiled and said that when Mary understood the situation, she would not only be willing but would want to. Mary would want Alex to share only the good news.

The two walked up the three sets of steps up to the porch and into the house.

Ron Mueller

Abandoned

Chapter 8: Linkages

In Brazil, Fernanda sat in her tiny three-room house. It was
all that she could afford because she was getting by on the
subsidy she got from social services. The money that Bento had
provided for a long time had run out and she got almost nothing
from the rest of her children. Until a year ago she and her
husband had enough to cover their living expenses. Now she was
at the point where she did not know what she would do in the
coming months to survive. She had spent her whole life cleaning
people's homes or doing the same in some hotel, but she now had
trouble standing for more than a short time. When her husband
was alive, and they were both working they always ended up
having enough to raise their large family. She thought about
sitting out on the sidewalk and begging. She was not sure that
would work without her getting in trouble with some gang that
would demand some of her money.

Ron Mueller

She wondered where Bento, his white wife and their mulatto daughter had gone. She had heard nothing, but she was sure that he was in hiding. She knew that he had been distributing drugs, so she figured that he was hiding from the police. She figured the fact that they had all disappeared meant that they were hiding so they could be together.

In Cincinnati, Aurea was expecting the worst news about her mother and father. It had been more than two weeks. She had followed the same routine of going to school and afterwards going to the library. She always made sure to attend some lecture that had refreshments. The lectures were usually interesting but what she really enjoyed was the afternoon treat.

Afterwards she would cruise the internet and spend some time improving her English. She especially like to use the map feature that let her go to anywhere in the world and be able to walk the streets in some foreign city.

The librarians all helped her select books to read. Once they found out that she did not want kids' books but books by famous authors they got her into reading books like Mark Twain's <u>Tom Sawyer</u>.

The internet had allowed her to check about missing persons and she learned that after forty-eight hours the missing person was most likely dead. Her parents were now missing for more than two weeks.

Abandoned

She liked Mary who was like a nanny to her but the person who she really admired was Alex. She treated her like an adult. She was kind and she was generous. They had gone out shopping and now she had a new bike, and she had several new outfits. She gone to her mother's house where she had gone fishing and got cooking lessons from Alex's mother.

She also liked Matt because he was fun to play with. She was learning how to play chess, they put together puzzles and he helped her do her homework. He seemed like a person who was fearless but was very gentle.

Getting her homework done was easy and even though she was the youngest in most of her classes she was at the head of most of her classes.

All three had gone out riding their bikes together. Her bike was amazing. It had six gears, hand brakes, front and rear suspension and it rode like a dream. Even the seat had its own suspension. She wondered how much it had cost but was afraid to ask. Alex had spent time with her and had explained how to check and replace the brake pads. She needed to do it often because she was constantly braking when going down the steep hills of Mt. Adams.

She had her own room that seemed like a small kingdom. Alex had told her that she was not rich but to her the house they lived in was amazing.

Ron Mueller

She had visited the third floor that had been turned into an art exhibit show room and was amazed to find various gorgeous paintings of local artists. The ones that really stood out were the paintings by Annie Scots an artist that when she looked her up on the internet, she found out she was very rich. Annie had been saved by Alex after being a chained prisoner in the woods for fifteen years. She now lived in Hawaii where she had met her husband. She had two daughters, Linda, and Lorie, who had gone to college and were now working in the family business.

She wanted to have her mother back but as the days passed, she felt that something bad had happened. She wondered what would happen to her if her mom and dad did not come back for her. She got on the internet and asked what happened to abandoned children. She learned about child social services where orphaned or abandoned children were sent. She knew that she did not want that to happen to her.

She had wondered whether Alex and Matt might be able to keep her. She knew that she had a grandmother in Brazil, but her grandmother was old, and she had never been nice to her. She did not want to go back to her grandmother or to Brazil.

She decided that she would have to wait until Alex found her mom and dad.

Abandoned

Alex had discussed her upcoming trip to Brazil with Matt. The two of them had agreed about going ahead with the adoption process if Aurea wanted that to happen. Alex said that the two of them should sit down with Aurea and share the sad news about her parents. Then they would let her know that the two of them wanted to adopt her. If Aurea had a positive response, then Alex, on her upcoming trip to Brazil would get the grandmother to sign the release that would allow the Brazilian adoption to take place. Once that was accomplished, they would also file the American adoption paperwork that her mother had prepared so that in the future the two of them would also have legal standing as parents in the US.

Getting the visas to go to Brazil was expedited but it took longer than Alex had anticipated because the visa was issued in New York.

The day before going to Brazil, Alex had Mary and Johnnie over for dinner. After dinner, Mary led Aurea into the living room where they all sat down. Mary led off by saying that she had sad news about her parents.

Aurea put up her hand and said that she knew the rest and didn't want to hear anything else.

Alex gave Aurea a hug and said that she was sorry about what had happened.

Aurea asked if she was going to be sent back to Brazil or have to go into the childcare system.

Alex asked if she wanted to go back to Brazil.

Aurea started crying and through her sobs, she said that she didn't want to, but she didn't want to go to child social services either.

Matt sat down next to her and asked if she would want to be adopted by him and Alex.

Aurea wiped away her tears and asked if that was possible.

Alex took out the adoption papers and showed her the Brazilian papers and gave her a chance to read them. Then she showed her the American adoption papers.

She said that she was going to Brazil and would get Aurea's grandmother to sign the papers. That would make Aurea her and Matt's daughter in Brazil. Once she got back, she and Matt would have a judge notarize the American adoption papers and they would become her legal parents in the US.

Aurea asked if she would lose her family name.

Alex asked what she wanted.

Aurea said that she would like to make her name Aurea Carvalho-Evercrest.

Alex wrote that down on the American adoption papers and said that would be the name on the American paperwork.

Aurea nodded and gave both Alex and Matt a hug. She then asked where her parents would be buried.

Alex said that they would find a nearby cemetery when she returned, and they would arrange for a burial service.

Abandoned

The following morning after seeing Aurea off to school with Mary, Alex rode with Johnnie down to the office. On the way he let her know that he was going to have her on camera when she went to the bar to arrest Cristiano. He said that he was sure that everyone in the office would be watching and cheering her on.

The Chief briefly called her into the office and said that he had contacted his Sao Paulo equivalent and arranged for the arrest of Cristiano. The two of them would be with the Brazilian team when the arrest was made. He smiled and said that he had done his best to ensure that she was the person making the arrest. He commented that he had received assurances that you would have all the backup that was warranted for that risky operation.

The Chief said that the Brazilian Chief there was very interested in making an arrest and was very pleased with the forensic information that Dr. Rogers had sent down. The arrest would be made by his officers when she confronted Cristiano. They would retrieve the tongue and ears and get them to the lab immediately and once confirmed they would lock Cristiano and his partner away for life.

Before they left the office the Chief once again cautioned them and told Trey to have her back.

Trevor made a smart-alecky remark to the effect that he knew Trey was a fearful guy and he would be glad to have her back and Trey could stay safe at home with his family.

Alex smiled and gave him her standard reply, "I love you too," and walked out with Trey to the waiting cab.

Ron Mueller

The flight to Brazil was on a new plane and the first-class seats were the new lay down style that felt like real beds. Alex spent a few moments sharing her adoption plans with Trey and then said that she planned to sleep all the way so that she would have all the energy she would need to make sure she got her two agenda items accomplished.

They arrived in Sao Paulo in the early morning hour. She and Trey both put on their Kevlar jackets beneath their sports jackets before deplaning. They were greeted as they got off the plane and were escorted to an office where they met the local Chief and after a brief introduction, he introduced a lady police officer, Lara, who was a Brazilian version of Alex in stature.

It was clear to Alex that the choice had been to match the two of them when she shook hands with Lara and then was introduced to her partner, João who was that same size as Trey. She liked the idea and was pleased that both of them spoke impeccable English. Having no language barriers going into a dangerous situation made her feel much better.

Lara explained that her unit was taking the lead but there would be a small army of police that would back them up. She and João would accompany Alex and Trey into the bar that was Cristiano and his partner's headquarters to make the arrest. They would be backed up internally by at least six additional police officers. There would be some thirty police surrounding the area. She handed both of them weapons that she asked not be used unless a gun fight was initiated by Cristiano or his partner.

Abandoned

Lara smiled and commented that Alex's gun fighting reputation was known to all of them and she was sure that if anything happened, she would make a difference so she should feel free to use her weapon if needed. She smiled again and repeated, "if needed."

Alex took off her jacket and put her weapon on and then put her jacket back on. She said that she felt at home and now she also felt ready to enter the lion's den.

Lara nodded and said that João would drive them to the bar and hopefully by late that evening they would all be enjoying dinner at her favorite Churrascaria and toasting, the arrest success and having two top drug dealers in prison, with a Caipirinha.

On the way Lara said that she had some protection vests in the trunk that they could use when they went into the bar.

Alex let her know that she and Trey already had their protection on.

Lara commented that she had not noticed it and wondered if it would hold up in a gun fight.

Alex nodded and said that both of them had survived multiple gunfights because of what they had on.

They arrived at the bar and were getting ready to enter. Alex noted that the external back-ups were all rushing into place and that everyone seemed to know what to do. She was pleased with the arrangements that had been made.

It was clear that they had surprised everyone sitting inside. Christiano and his partner were sitting at a table just in front of the bar. As soon as they realized it was a raid, they both dropped to the floor, drew their weapons, and began firing.

Alex drew her weapon and fired just as she was hit in the side by Cristiano. She stood her ground and her shot hit him in between the eyes. She then turned and began to strategically shoot anyone that was firing a weapon. She knew that Trey was firing and doing the same.

The room had seemed to explode. She shot the bartender as he raised a shotgun. Trey was standing beside her, and they both emptied their weapons and took out someone each time they fired. The room went quiet as fast as it had exploded into a storm of gunfire.

The number of police seemed to mushroom as the room went silent and the remaining members of Cristiano's gang that were still alive were hand cuffed and led away. There were several that were wounded and were being attended to.

Lara and João came over to them and commented that they had never seen two people that were so deadly.

Lara's eyes went wide when she noticed the bullet hole in Alex's jacket. She asked if she was OK.

Alex said that she was going to have a large bruise that would be painful for a few days but otherwise she would be fine. She was sad to have lost another jacket but that was easily replaced.

Abandoned

She added that she planned to handle it like all the other times she had been hit. She hoped that taking some pain killer and time in the hot tub would be enough.

João pointed to a hole in Trey's jacket and asked what type of bullet proof vest the two were using because he was interested in getting something similar.

Trey commented that it was the type that had kept the two of them alive through multiple gun battles.

Lara walked over to where the EMT's were treating the wounded. She returned with two tubes of salve that she said would help ease the pain.

Back in Cincinnati the morning was just underway when the action began, the Chief, Dr. Rogers, Johnnie, Bill, and Trevor sat with their morning cups of coffee and their donuts as if they were going to the movies. They viewed the entire situation from just before Alex and the police arrived.

They all gasped when Cristiano and his partner immediately started firing. It caught all of them by surprise, but they noticed the immediate reaction by Alex and Trey. They were firing before any of the Brazilian police had even drawn their weapons.

Then they watched the amazing, synchronized gun display that Alex and Trey put on. The two seemed to be demonstrating a shooting dance routine. The two of them took out all but two of the gunmen before any of the other police even began to fire. The yelling and cheering in the conference room attracted the entire squad. They all came over to the conference room window to see what was happening.

Johnnie looked at the Chief and asked if he should play the gunfight scene again and got the nod to do so. The Chief invited everyone in and explained what had just happened. The reaction of the rest of the department mirrored the reaction of the smaller group. During the second viewing Johnnie commented that he thought both Alex and Trey had had been hit by the first two shots but had continued firing until their guns were empty.

Bill agreed and said that they would both be sitting in the hot tub that evening. He recalled having done that several time when all of them hand been hit.

The Chief said that he was treating everyone to lunch in celebration of what Alex and Trey had just done.

Abandoned

Lara came over and asked that Alex and Trey give her their weapons and act like they never had them. She explained that the weapons and anyone that had used them would have to explain why they used them to the police internal affairs division. She and João would claim that they had used the weapons otherwise Alex and Trey would be stuck in Brazil for many days in some stuffy office.

Alex thanked her but Lara laughed. She said that Alex's and Trey's shooting would make she and João famous for their ability to kill the two leading drug dealers in Sao Paulo and most of his inner circle. They were likely to get promoted and get a raise.

Alex laughed and said that she was glad to help.

That evening at the Churrascaria Lara's Chief called for a toast to his two top gun slingers and their American partners. Alex raised her non-alcohol Caipirinha and joined the toast. She said that she and Trey had a gift for their two partners. She handed Lara a package that had her Kevlar outfit in it and said that if it didn't fit, she would send down another one. Trey did the same and gave a package to João. The two of them had agreed that not having to face the Brazilian equivalent of internal affairs made the gifts seem a pittance.

During the dinner, Alex asked Lara if she would accompany her the next day so that she could get some adoption papers signed.

Lara asked about the situation and commented that her boss had the ears and tongue of the person that Cristiano had killed and was having the DNA compared to that sent to him by Dr. Rogers.

She now understood why Alex had come down to make the arrest and she would take it as an honor to help her get the adoption papers signed.

Alex made an excuse to everyone at the celebration about needing to get ready for the next day and she and Trey left.

When they got back to the hotel, she said that she was going to sit in the hot tub.

Trey said that he would join her.

When they got to the tub it was clear that each of them was going to sport a significant bruise on the right side of their ribs.

The next morning, Lara and João met them and drove them to the address where Fernanda lived. Alex had explained her goal and had asked Lara to come in with her.

Joao said they were in a neighborhood that having them stay to watch the car was a good idea.

Lara was dressed in basic black and looked like a partner to Alex. They knocked on the door and asked if they could enter. After a brief introduction, Alex, through Lara, shared that both Janaina and Bento were dead.

Abandoned

She then shared the fact she wanted to adopt Aurea. It was clear to her that Fernanda did not want to take Aurea in, but she was sharp enough to bargain for something in exchange. Alex made her first compensation offer on the low side and after a series of offers and counter offers, she hit the amount that she had Johnnie put into the bank branch that was closest to the address where Fernanda lived.

She had Fernanda sign the adoption paperwork and had Lara sign as a witness. She handed Fernanda the account booklet and let her know that a similar amount would be put in every month for the rest of her life.

Fernanda thanked her and wished her well. She felt a sense of relief to have enough to live on and not to have to raise another child. She felt certain that Aurea would be much better off with the person who had spent the time to come to meet with her and was willing to give her money to adopt her.

Lara walked out and complemented Alex on her bargaining skills and asked if she had gotten what she needed and the dollar amount that she had wanted to hit.

Alex gave Lara a hug and said that everything had come out as she wanted. She had gained a daughter and the amount she had agreed to was almost to the dollar what she had planned. Having Lara there to translate had made the meeting the success she needed.

Lara laughed and said that she had been worried that Alex would be out bargained but it had become clear to her by the way the bargaining went that Alex had the upper hand. She asked when had she set up the bank account and how had she done it from outside the country.

Alex said that she had a magician that she was able to leverage to get most things in the world done.

Trey was standing and listening to the exchange and said that Alex attacked everything in the same manner that she shot her weapon. She hit the bullseye every time.

Lara nodded and said that the preliminary autopsies indicated that the two of them had killed most of the shooters. Christiano and his partner had their bullets in them and the remaining bullets from their weapons had killed every person that they hit, and they had not doubled up on any of them.

The coroner had praised her and João for their exceptional marksmanship. He said that he was making sure his report would go to the top department leaders. Lara went on to say that she and João were sure to get a lot of recognition, probably a pay raise and very likely a promotion for what had occurred during the gun battle.

Alex laughed and said that she hoped the two of them would indeed get promoted and if either of them decided to come to the states they should come to Cincinnati, and she would host them.

The next day, Alex and Trey were on their way back home.

Chapter 9: Arrangements

On their return Alex immediately called John and asked him to contact her mother and arrange to proceed with the adoption. John said he knew the judge that he would recommend, would talk with Alex's mother, and arranged for it to happen. He said that he was so glad to be involved and thanked her.

Alex had another matter that affected Aurea that she had promised to take care of. She had returned with Bento's missing pieces which she took to Dr. Rogers.

He commented that he had watched the gun fight and that everyone had watched her, and Trey display their synchronized gunmanship. Even though he knew that the gunfight had been started by Christiano he said they seemed to have practiced that event and it looked as if they were firing and moving in rhythm. He said that he also thought both of them had been hit but it appeared that neither had gotten any medical attention.

Alex admitted that both of them had been hit but their Kevlar jackets had protected them, and they did not want to get held up with follow up medical attention or face the Brazilian internal affairs division.

Ron Mueller

Dr. Rogers shook his head and added that the entire department had by now seen the shootout and she and Trey were both legends. He added that the Chief had let him know that practice on the gun range had skyrocketed.

Alex asked Dr. Rogers about arranging the burial.

He suggested a mortuary she should use so that she could get arrangements made to handle the ceremony.

That evening she asked Aurea whether she wanted to have an open coffin ceremony.

Aurea shook her head and said no but she wanted the family picture that had the three of them standing together made big and have that be what was on display during the ceremony.

Alex was glad that was the choice.

She went to mortuary that had been recommended and made the arrangements.

The ceremony was held on the weekend and was attended by the entire team. It was a simple one and the trip to the cemetery was only a short few blocks away and everyone walked to the burial site. Alex had selected the site that was only a mile away from her house. She wanted to make it easy for Aurea to visit it if she desired to do so.

She was worried that Aurea was holding her grief in and asked her if she wanted to talk to anyone about her feelings. Aurea said that she had talked about how she felt with Mary and had been asked the same question. She said that she was sad and at the same time she was happy and that made her feel guilty.

Abandoned

Alex said she had just the person that would help her talk through those feelings. She said that what the two of them talked about would only be between them.

She arranged for the therapist that the whole team used and set up a time after school that Aurea could meet with her. She personally had gone and talked with her several times in the last few weeks and knew that she would help Aurea work through her feelings.

The next thing she happily focused her energy on was arranging the adoption. She sent out the invitation to family, friends, Aurea's teachers, and the librarians at the downtown library.

She, Matt, and Aurea walked down the aisle passed a packed gallery that had every person that she had invited present. The Chief and Rose Anne, Bill and his wife, Trevor and his wife, Trey, Leslie, and Nolan, Annie, Brian, Linda and Laurie and Annie's parents, Kekoa Ikaika and his wife Anela Kamaka, Brian's parents, Brenda Langley, her art studio partner and Johnnie and Mary, her mother and father, Jane, the Illinois Lieutenant Governor, Dexter, the owner of the Golden Goose, Sandra Olsen, her one time police woman guard, Harold Zimmerman and his Chicago DEA team, Andy Weller the Chicago IRS head, Joe Brown Cincinnati IRS leader, Randolf Task, the Texas IRS leader, James Kaizer, Sheriff of Wiggin Mississippi and his wife and kids, Angelica, the Angel on the Hill and her brother and his wife, Cais Leu her long time Vietnamese college friend, Evin Williams the Loveland Sheriff and his wife Irene, Brian Lexter the Cincinnati FBI bureau chief and his wife, were all sitting in the gallery.

The surprise was that all the teachers in Aurea's school and the librarians from the downtown public library were all in the gallery as well.

The gallery was packed and there was standing room only.

Alex had invited all of them to a celebration at the restaurant where a few years earlier Alex had shot and killed the thug that had come to kill Johnnie. The owner of the restaurant was ecstatic about being chosen to host the celebration and made a special point of letting them all know that Alex was one of the persons that had made the restaurant so successful. Alex smiled as she thought about the fact that she might have a few more people than she had estimated. She hoped the restaurant was up to it.

The three of them walked slowly down to the table where John and Hanna were waiting for them and sat at a table with the two of them to face the Judge's desk. When the court bailiff called the court to order, everyone in the court room stood up. Judge Kimberly Nugent, the same judge who had presided in the "Slate" case entered, sat down behind the bench, and in a very formal and serious tone asked the courtroom deputy to administer the oath to the three very lucky people sitting before her. She had a big smile on her face as she asked the judicial clerk to read the adoption request.

Abandoned

None of this was actually necessary. They could have met in her office and had the paperwork signed, but she and John had decided to make it a formal court affair.

She then asked Aurea if she wanted to be the daughter of Alex and Matt. When she got a simple yes. She asked why she would want that to happen.

Aurea stood and in a quiet but clear voice said that her parents had taken her to Alex's and Matt's house and told her that she had been brought there because they knew that Alex would keep her safe from the bad people that were after them. They had faith that they were putting her on the porch of someone that they trusted. Aurea looked at Alex and Matt and then went on to add that she had felt their love and wanted them to be her parents. She was going to be able to keep her biological family name and add Evercrest at the end.

They had found a nearby cemetery and had made sure her biological parents received a proper burial. She would miss her mother and father, but she knew that she was with the two people that she would be very happy to call mother and father. She had tears running down her face as she finished her reply.

Alex and Matt, both gave her a hug.

The Judge Nugent smiled as she signed the paperwork, handed it to John, pronounced Alex and Matt the parents of Aurea and then slammed her gavel down and declared court dismissed.

There was a loud cheer as she came around from the judge's desk to the table where Alex and Matt were giving Aurea a hug and said that she was so happy that she had been the one given the privilege to make it all official.

Everyone in the court room came down from the gallery onto the main floor and gathered around giving hugs and congratulations.

Alex stood back from the crowd as she thought about the fact that she felt that she had been given the best wish that she could possibly have been granted.

Her mother gave her a hug and quietly said, "It's a little overwhelming "I know that it is not only what you wished would happen but as you can see everyone that knows you wanted to be here to see you get your wish."

Alex nodded and said that she was glad that there was time for all of them to walk to the park so she could have time to decompress.

The gathering at the restaurant was a huge success. The music in the background had been selected by Aurea and was upbeat and had featured violin, piano and viola pieces. This was in contrast to the more somber music that she had selected for her parents commemoration service. Alex noted the difference of the music selection between the two events and felt very good about it. She was also impressed with Aurea's depth of musical expertise.

Abandoned

The celebration went well into the night and afterwards she, Matt, Aurea, Johnnie, and Mary all walked up the hill to Mt. Adams.

The next day there was a much smaller gathering at her house. Her parents were staying for a couple of days as were Annie, Brian, Linda, and Laurie and Kekoa Ikaika and his wife Anela Kamaka, Brian's parents. She had invited Annie's parents and Trey, Lesley, and Nolan as well for the backyard grill out.

Aurea confided to her that she was a little overwhelmed by the way everyone had congratulated her on getting the best parents that she possibly could have gotten.

Alex chuckled and said that she would remind her of that when they got into a disagreement. She said that she would just say, "the best parents ever."

The End

Ron Mueller

Abandoned

About the Author

Ronald E. Mueller
remwriter95@gmail.com

Ron grew up in what is now Flint River State Park in Southeast Iowa. The 170-year-old house Ron lived in is built into a hillside. It faces a 125-foot-high cliff towering over the little Flint River. The house and the land talked to him about; the passing of time, the struggle to conquer the land, the struggles people faced and the wonder of nature.

He climbed the cliffs, crawled into the caves, dove from the swimming rock, collected clams from the bottom of the pond, gigged and skinned frogs for their legs. He trapped muskrats for fur, hunted raccoon in the dead of night, and with only a stick hunted rabbits in the dead of winter.

His young life was outdoors, and nature tested him.

He walked to a one room stone schoolhouse uphill both ways. A stern but warm-hearted teacher, Mrs. Henry was instrumental in shaping his character as she shepherded him from the fourth to the eighth grade. A Montessori before its time. It was a great way to grow up.

His experiences inter-twined with snippets of fantasy lend themselves to the adventures he leads the reader through.

Ron Mueller

<u>Characters in the Story</u>

Alex	Cathy	Evercrest	Police Detective
Matthew	Timothy	Knolton	Alex's suitor
Rose-Anne	Germain	Evercrest	Alex's mother
Russel	Johnson	Evercrest	Alex's father
Helping Hands charity			Alex's nonprofit org
Trey		McGregor	Alex's Detective Partner
Lindsey		McGregor	Wife
Nolan		McGregor	Son
Johnnie		Smith	Old Viet Vet
Mary		Higgins	Johnnie's Phili "friend"
Bruce	Lincoln	Johnson	Cinci Chief of Detectives
Mary-Anne	Leslie	Johnson	Chiefs Wife
Bill	Hamilton	Danson	Detective
Travis	Bailey	Carter	Detective
Dr. Rogers			Coroner
Jane	Elousie	Stradford	Lieutenant Governor
Felix			proprietor at fishing dock
Golden Goose			Name of the Yacht
Sandra		Olson	Policewoman guard
Annie	Lorie	Scots	Missing girl
Linda		Annies	older daughter
Lorie		Annies	second daughter
Harold		Zimmerman	Chicago DEA
James	Oscor	Kaizer	Sheriff of Wiggin
Abbie	Alisa	Bender	married James
John	S.	Williams	Lawyer was abused
Hanna		Waverly	John's mate
Angelica			Angel on the hill
Brian		Lexter	FBI Bureau Chief
Cais		Leu	Alex's Viet friend
Tracy		Hunter	Trey's Analyst

<u>Abandoned</u>

Bento		Carvalho	Father
Janaina		Carvalho	Mother
Aurea		Carvalho	Abandoned
Cristiano			
Fernanda		Carvalho	Grandmother
Lara			Woman officer Braz
João			Police officer Brazil

Abandoned

Published by: Around the World Publishing LLC.

QR Links to
ATWP.US web site

www.ingramcontent.com/pod-product-compliance
Lightning Source LLC
Chambersburg PA
CBHW060555100726
47907CB00005B/1374